'Would you like me to assist?' he asked, hoping she'd refuse.

Ivy positively beamed, and took a step forward. For a moment she wore such a supreme look of relief that he thought she might kiss him.

He wouldn't have minded. In fact, just the possibility of feeling her lips against his sent blood rushing through his body. Having such a strong physical reaction on the basis of merely *thinking* about a kiss plainly indicated he'd been alone for too long.

Jessica Matthews's interest in medicine began at a young age, and she nourished it with medical stories and hospital-based television programmes. After a stint as a teenage candy-striper, she pursued a career as a clinical laboratory scientist. When not writing or on duty, she fills her day with countless family and school-related activities. Jessica lives in the central United States, with her husband, daughter and son.

Recent titles by the same author:

THE ROYAL DOCTOR'S BRIDE

THE
BABY DOCTOR'S
BRIDE

BY
JESSICA MATTHEWS

MILLS & BOON™

Pure reading pleasure™

All the characters in this book have no existence outside the imagination of the author, and have no relation whatsoever to anyone bearing the same name or names. They are not even distantly inspired by any individual known or unknown to the author, and all the incidents are pure invention.

First published in Great Britain 2009
Harlequin Mills & Boon Limited,
Eton House, 18-24 Paradise Road, Richmond, Surrey TW9 1SR

© Jessica Matthews 2009

ISBN: 978 0 263 86842 5

Set in Times Roman 10½ on 12¼ pt
03-0509-51047

Printed and bound in Spain
by Litografia Rosés, S.A., Barcelona

THE
BABY DOCTOR'S
BRIDE

To my family, whose unwavering support has been my inspiration.

CHAPTER ONE

DESPERATE times called for desperate measures.

Ivy Harris parked her SUV on the circular gravel driveway in front of the hunting lodge commonly known as the old Beckett place. For a moment she clutched the steering wheel in a white-knuckled grip as she studied her surroundings.

The rustic house, built to resemble a log cabin, was nestled in a shady grove of cottonwood and oak trees. According to her father, the building sat on the edge of three hundred and twenty acres of private land, teeming with deer, quail and turkeys, and was a popular rental property during the hunting season. But she didn't care about the house or the land or the wildlife. She was only interested in the lodge's current resident.

After inhaling a bracing breath for courage, she slid out from the behind the wheel. There was no sign of human life— no vehicles, open windows or tools scattered around the yard—and she wondered if today's excursion was simply a wasted effort. But she'd come too far to jump to conclusions. If Ethan Locke wasn't here now he would eventually return, and she would be waiting.

Provided he didn't take longer than her scheduled lunch break.

Her trainers crunched eerily against the gravel as she tramped up the path toward the front concrete steps, conscious of the birds merrily chirping overhead and two squirrels playing tag in the uppermost branches. For an instant she chided herself for not taking time to spruce herself up a bit, in an effort to give a good first impression, but in the next she was glad she hadn't. She hadn't come to make a fashion statement, with her khaki trousers, the yellow tank top with its faint pink stains courtesy of a small patient's cherry lollipop, and her tennis shoes. Looking like the frazzled physician she was, rather than a woman ready for an afternoon of tea parties and shopping, could only help her cause—or so she hoped.

Determined to be as eloquent and as convincing as possible, she pounded on the weathered screen door.

No one responded.

She tested the screen door and found it unlatched. This time she pounded on the inside door.

Still no answer.

Slowly she closed the screen door and glanced at her watch. She could stay another fifteen minutes, but any longer than that would throw off her schedule. If her afternoon passed like most of them had, she'd be working until well past dinner.

Still, it couldn't be helped. She sat on the front step and stretched out her legs. Without warning, a tall, chocolate-brown-haired man in his late thirties rounded the corner of the cabin, carrying a fifty-pound bag of birdseed over his shoulder. In spite of his rather disreputable state—ragged denim jeans, stained T-shirt, tousled hair and unshaven face—his lean physique and muscled chest made him worthy of a second glance.

Considering how it had been ages since she'd given any man another look, she was surprised by how easily this one had momentarily made her forget her purpose for being there.

"Hi," she said brightly, jumping to her feet.

He dropped the bag next to a bird feeder in the front yard with a thump and straightened. His storm-cloud-blue gaze was direct, and his straight nose, square jaw, and well-defined cheekbones formed a breathtakingly handsome face. "Hello," he said, in a deep, pleasant voice. "I hope you're not lost and looking for directions, because I haven't lived here long enough to be helpful."

"I'm not," she assured him. "I'm here because I'm looking for Ethan Locke."

Suspicion instantly replaced his welcoming smile. "What do you want with him?"

"It's personal. Do you know where he is?"

He hesitated for several seconds, as if unwilling to answer. "I'm Ethan Locke," he finally said.

Impossible. She'd been told the man was retired, so this had to be his son. "I'm looking for *Dr.* Ethan Locke," she stressed as she walked toward his side.

"In the flesh," he answered gruffly.

"*You're* Dr. Locke?" she asked, startled by his admission because she'd been expecting a much older man.

"Yeah, and who wants to know?"

The congenial man she'd first encountered had become a gruff, taciturn fellow. "Ivy Harris," she said in her most friendly manner, although from his frown her effort was wasted. "I have to apologize," she continued. "I'd been told you'd retired so I'd expected someone..."

"Gray-haired and walking with a cane?" he finished dryly.

Her face warmed. "Not quite. In any case," she pressed on, "rumor says you're a doctor. A pediatrician, in fact."

"Not anymore. According to you I'm retired, remember?" He slit one corner of the bag with a utility knife, then began pouring birdseed into the feeder. "Did you want something in particular, or did you just drop by to interrupt my peaceful morning?"

For some reason referring to his profession had pressed one of his hot buttons, but she'd come too far to give up now. While she would have preferred to state her case with his undivided attention, she couldn't demand he stop what he was doing when she *had* arrived unexpectedly and without an invitation. "I have a proposition for you."

"A proposition?" He paused to rake an insolent gaze along her full length. "I'm flattered, but I'd rather not spend my days in jail."

Her face warmed with embarrassment in spite of the shade-cooled breeze. "Not that sort of proposition," she said loftily. "A *business* proposition."

"Doesn't matter what sort it is. My answer is no."

"But you haven't heard the details. The least you can do is listen. Please?" Trying not to beg, she added, "It's important."

"It always is," he mumbled, before he set the bag of seed on the ground, reattached the lid to the feeder, and strode toward the cabin's front door. "I suppose you'd better come inside."

It wasn't the most gracious welcome, but he was willing to hear her out, so she'd find her victories wherever she could.

In spite of his gruff manner, he courteously held open the screen door for her. "Thanks," she murmured, equally polite.

As soon as she stepped across the threshold into the main living area she instantly felt at home. Because she spent nearly all of her day seeing patients in claustrophobic cubicles, open spaces appealed to her. If she had a place like this to come home to every night, she'd be one happy lady.

"This is quite impressive," she said, taking in the rough-hewn log walls, the flagstone fireplace, the bear rug in front of a leather sofa and the overall "Southwest" interior design. At the opposite end of the great room stood an old oak table, large enough to accommodate eight comfortably, and a kitchen area that boasted modern appliances.

Furnishings aside, Ethan Locke dominated the space.

He clicked off the television, then crossed to the table, where a half-empty bottle of water stood, and drank deeply. "I'm sure you didn't drive this far off the beaten path to discuss my accommodations," he said when he'd finished.

"No, I didn't," she said, refusing to be intimidated by every inch of his six feet plus lean frame or the frown on his ruggedly bewhiskered face. "I need your help."

"Oh?" Everything about him exuded skepticism, from the way he folded his arms across his massive chest to the suspicion shining in his blue-gray eyes.

"Actually, the whole town needs you."

He raised one eyebrow. "Somehow I find that hard to believe."

"It's true," she insisted. "With our only family practitioner, Walt Griffith, gone—"

"What happened to him?"

"Nothing, but his brother in Phoenix had a stroke and he went to visit. Apparently he's not doing well, and Walt thinks he could pass on anytime, so he doesn't want to leave. Which is okay because a friend of his, Jed Richardson, has taken over."

"Then I don't see a problem."

"Jed's an internist, which means I've inherited all of Walt's pediatric patients. I'm a pediatrician, too, by the way."

"Lucky you."

She ignored his comment, although she wondered at the reason for his attitude. "To make matters worse, I have seven kids with whooping cough."

He frowned. "Aren't you encouraging your parents to vaccinate their children? Or don't they teach that in med school these days?"

"The ink may not be quite dry on my board certification," she ground out, irritated by how easily he'd jumped to the wrong conclusions. She could quickly imagine what he'd think if he knew she'd moved here less than a month ago. "But Walt and I are both well aware of the importance of childhood vaccinations. Three of my cases are eight years and older, and are current with their shots. The other four are babies who haven't received the full immunization regimen yet. They aren't sick because of parental or physician negligence."

He let out a deep sigh and stroked his face thoughtfully with one hand, which wasn't an apology, but a reluctant acknowledgment of his wrong assumptions.

"What do you want from me?" he asked in a more modulated tone.

Hope rose and Ivy stepped closer. "Your help," she answered promptly. "Your hands. Your expertise. I'm working twenty-four hour days, and I can't be effective if I continue at this pace. It isn't fair to my patients."

"Hire a locum."

"I've tried, but no one's available until the end of the summer. You, on the other hand, are here and—" she met his dark-eyed gaze "—available."

"I'm on vacation."

"For how long?"

"Indefinitely. Think of me as being on sabbatical—which means I'm not sitting on the back porch, birdwatching."

Picturing his huge bag of birdseed, she suspected he was, but it would be rude to correct him. She couldn't risk alienating him more than she apparently already had. "Regardless of how you describe your stay, technically you're free."

"It means I'm not punching a clock or taking orders from someone else," he countered. "And I'm not going to."

She eyed him carefully, irritated by his refusal, and desperate to gain his cooperation. "Give me one good reason why you won't help."

"I don't want to."

"Not good enough."

"What if I said I was sick?"

She gave him a quick once-over, noting how casually he stood straight and tall on muscular legs. His biceps and forearms were well developed, too, as if he lifted weights on a regular basis. He'd also carried a fifty-pound bag across the yard with the easy grace and sure footing of a panther. While he didn't have the deep tan of someone who spent his days in the sun, he certainly didn't possess the washed-out, pale color of someone who either was or had been ill.

The only thing she could say about him was that he looked like a man on vacation—a man who hadn't taken time to shave that morning, a man whose thick hair was longer than she guessed he usually allowed it to be. But underneath the grubby look she saw a tall, suave, sophisticated man in his late thirties, who had an intensely serious expression capable of drawing women to him like metal shavings to a magnet if he'd only smile. Or smile more often.

"I wouldn't believe you," she said smartly. "According to Lew at the gas station, you're retired."

"He's wrong."

"Obviously," she said dryly. "So you came to Danton for a vacation, but—"

"An extended and well-deserved vacation is what I intend to have. Find someone else if you need an extra pair of hands."

"There *isn't* anyone else," she insisted. "Look, if you want to spend your days resting and relaxing, great. But can't you spare a few weeks out of your *busy* schedule? I'm not asking you to work twenty-hour days, either. Nine to four, Monday through Friday. I'll take care of the night and weekend call schedule."

Her offer was quite generous, in her opinion, but if he wanted more—such as working only three days a week—she'd agree to his terms, because any assistance he could give was better than none.

"I sympathize with you, but I'm not interested."

"I'll pay you a salary," she offered impulsively.

He raised one dark eyebrow. "You said this is your first practice?"

"Yeah, so?"

"Then you don't have two cents to rub together." His tone was flat. "I know because I've been there myself. Unless you're independently wealthy?"

"I'm not. If you won't accept a salary, then I'll split the office profits with you, with none of the expenses." She didn't know how she'd manage that and still meet her loan payments, but she'd find a way.

"I don't take advantage of my colleagues," he stated. "Save your money."

Calling her a colleague boosted Ivy's hopes for the second time since she'd walked into the cabin. "Then it's a deal? You'll join me?"

"No."

Impatiently, she rubbed the back of her neck and struggled to hold her tone even. "What's the problem?"

"There isn't a problem. I just want to be left alone," he ground out. "Is that too difficult a concept for you to grasp, Dr. Harris?"

Although the red highlights in her hair came courtesy of her hairdresser, Ivy's temper rose to match. "You don't have a concept. You have an *excuse*. How can you ignore children who need a doctor?"

"They have you, and you seem capable enough."

"What about your Hippocratic Oath and the joy of healing those who seek your help?"

"I can't help you, Dr. Harris," he said flatly.

"You won't," she corrected.

"I have my reasons."

"Which are?"

"None of your business, Dr. Harris."

"Perhaps you don't understand the dynamics of rural communities. Everyone helps each other. Think on that the next time you go to town and expect someone to serve you at the diner, sack and carry your groceries, or change the oil in your car."

"For the record, I'm immune to threats."

"A threat would be if I said no one would serve you," she said through gritted teeth. "I'm merely pointing out that the people in this area share their skills and talents. We don't hoard or use them only when it's convenient." Her voice shook with frustration. "You don't have any children, do you, Dr. Locke?"

His eyes turned dark and his expression cold. "No."

"I didn't think so, because if you did, I wonder how *you'd* feel if you had a sick son or daughter and the doctor who could treat him refused because his vacation was more important."

He didn't answer.

Unable to spend another minute in his presence, she headed for the exit. "Enjoy your rest and relaxation, *Doctor*. I hope you'll be very happy spending time in your ivory tower."

She stormed out, carefully and quietly closing the screen

door when it was tempting to do the opposite. It was equally tempting to rev her engine and scatter the gravel as she peeled out of the driveway, but she refused to act in such a petty manner. Ethan Locke might think of her as a country hick, but she possessed more class than that. With any luck she wouldn't run into the man for the rest of his so-called vacation, however long it lasted. Considering how she spent nearly all of her time at the clinic, the ten-bed hospital, or her father's diner, the odds of never seeing him again lay solidly in her favor.

Twenty minutes later she parked in her spot behind the Danton clinic's employee entrance and gratefully entered the air-conditioned wing which had been earmarked for pediatrics.

Heather Fox, Ivy's office nurse and inseparable childhood friend, poked her head out of an exam room as Ivy walked past. "How did it go?"

Ivy detoured into the cubicle and sank into a chair. "Not well. He turned me down. Flatly and unequivocally. I shouldn't be surprised or disappointed. It was a long shot."

Long shot or not, she'd carried high hopes… To add insult to injury, it wasn't fair for a man with his good looks to be such a selfish grump! What an insult to pediatricians everywhere!

"Hmm. I would have thought a retired gent would have been happy to hop back into the saddle and supplement his income for a few weeks."

"He's not retired," Ivy said. "I don't know how Lew got that impression, but Ethan Locke hasn't hit forty. To quote him, he's on 'an extended and well-deserved vacation'."

"He's under forty and can take an extended holiday? Wow! Makes you wonder what *his* rates as a pediatrician are."

Remembering how he'd related to Ivy's lack of finances, she wondered that herself. If he'd earned his millions by charging his patients exorbitant fees, it was a good thing he'd turned her down. Neither she nor the families in the area could afford his services. "No kidding."

Heather frowned, clearly puzzling out the situation. "So why did he say no? Even if he's wealthy, I'd think he'd be willing to volunteer."

"'Let me count the ways'," Ivy quoted as she began ticking off his reasons on her fingers. "He's on vacation. He's not interested. He wants to be left alone."

"Did you explain he wouldn't have any evening or week-end duty?"

"I did, but he still wasn't interested." Ivy pinched the bridge of her nose. "Nothing I said made a difference." She met her friend's gaze, disappointed by her failure. "I'm sorry, Heather. I know you'd like to leave at a decent time every evening to spend time with your family, and now—"

"Hey, don't apologize. You did everything you could." She sighed. "This hasn't been the best welcome home for you, either, Ivy. Instead of a quiet summer with Dr. Griffith, getting to know the routine, you got tossed in over your head from the very beginning."

Ivy shrugged, although she smiled. "Don't worry about me. Murphy's Law and medicine seem to go hand in hand. We'll do the best we can and hope it's enough."

Like all other doctors, she'd learned how to function without sleep, and how to survive on a few winks grabbed here and there, but as an intern and as a resident at Children's Mercy, there had always been medical people around to catch any blatant errors she might make. Here, she didn't have a safety net.

Ethan Locke was the nearest candidate, and he wasn't interested. Still, no point in crying over circumstances that couldn't be changed.

"I just hate to ask you to work such long days when you have your own pre-schoolers at home," Ivy continued.

The nurse shrugged. "This situation won't last forever. My mother loves babysitting, and I doubt if the kids miss Mom all that much when Grandma caters to their every whim."

"Believe me, when things get back to normal, I'll insist on you taking time off."

"I won't argue over that," Heather said with a smile. "But if you ask me, you're the one I'm worried about. When's the last time you slept?"

Ivy thought back. "I got a few hours last night." Those had come between two-year-old Erica Weyland's asthma attack and five-year-old Tabitha Jones's sprained wrist after she'd fallen out of her new canopy twin bed.

"And when did you eat last?"

Ivy tried to remember. Breakfast seemed like such a long time ago. "I grabbed a cinnamon roll from the hospital cafeteria this morning."

"Then it's a good thing your dad sent over a take-out order of his meatloaf special. It's in the lounge with your name on it."

Ivy's mouth watered, but her wristwatch told her it would have to wait. "I'll eat later."

"You'll eat it now," Heather ordered. "The kids can wait ten more minutes to see you, especially if it means their doctor won't collapse from hunger. So go, put up your feet for a few minutes, and don't come back until you've cleaned your plate."

Ivy didn't argue. "Yes, Mother," she said, grateful that her father, once again, had come to her rescue.

At least there were some good men in this world, she thought uncharitably as a mental picture of Ethan Locke appeared. It probably was a good thing he'd turned her down, because he might be handsome and he might be talented, but he clearly didn't have a heart.

Ethan slumped onto the sofa and stared at the blank television screen, wishing the bottle in his hand held something more bracing than water.

When he'd first laid eyes on his surprise guest, he'd been dazzled. The easy way she moved, the apparent softness of her skin, the shine to her shoulder-length auburn hair, the impish smile on her beautiful face had made him feel as if the sun had reappeared in his life after months of cloudy days.

And for the first time in a long time he'd also been curious. During the few weeks he'd been living here no one, not even the mail carrier, had wandered down his lane. For a man who'd been content to mark the days by the number of soda pop bottles he emptied, curiosity was a novel experience.

Then she'd started asking questions, discussing things he didn't want to discuss. One visit that could have held some promise and make him feel "normal" had suddenly ruined his day. Hell, she'd ruined his entire week!

Almost six months ago he'd left his life behind in St. Louis. After severing the few ties he had in the Gateway City, he'd packed the belongings he couldn't live without in his car and stored the rest. He'd headed west on I-70 without any clear-cut destination in mind other than a desire to find a quiet location to settle until he refocused his life.

His criteria had been simple. He'd wanted a place where he would be as average as the next guy, a place where no one would expect more from him than he was willing to give, a place where he could sort out his life and find peace. A place where he could forget....

Surprisingly enough, a place meeting his specifications had been more difficult to find than he'd expected, but after detouring off one interstate onto another that headed south, he'd stumbled across Danton, a southern Kansas town of about five thousand, which provided enough retail businesses and services to satisfy its residents. Healthcare was limited to a doctor and a ten-bed hospital that was equipped to deal with emergencies and provide nursing care for anyone needing round-the-clock attention they couldn't receive at home. Thanks to a conversation with the loose-lipped Lew, who'd obviously found the doctor's parking permit Ethan had yanked off the rearview mirror and shoved under the driver's seat, he'd hunted down the owner of this cabin, signed a lease and moved in for the summer.

He'd taken to his new surroundings without any problem, and knew he'd made the right choice to leave his old life. After nearly six months of drifting, he didn't miss the phones ringing, his pager buzzing, the monitors beeping, the gentle whoosh of respirators, or babies that fit in the palm of his hand. More importantly, he didn't miss the worry, the tears, or the sense of failure.

Allowing each minute, each hour, to pass by quietly and without plan or purpose seemed therapeutic, although he didn't expect to be healed of what ailed him.

How did one recover from disillusionment, especially when you were disillusioned with yourself?

I need your help.

She might need help, but she didn't need his, he thought sourly. He was the last doctor she'd want treating her precious patients, although she didn't know that. Better for her to think he was a selfish bastard, that he had no heart, than for her to know the truth.

Actually, knowing she hung at the end of her emotional rope bothered him more than he cared to admit—mainly because he'd been there, done that. If only she'd stayed away;

if only Lew hadn't discovered Ethan was a doctor; if only he had chosen today to pack a lunch and explore the acres and acres surrounding the cabin. Then he could have remained in ignorant isolation.

But she hadn't left him in peace. In a few short minutes she'd done what his colleagues in St. Louis hadn't been able to accomplish in months.

She'd made him feel guilty.

Feeling guilty was a step up from feeling like a failure, which was how he'd felt in the weeks before he left St. Louis. Like Dr. Harris, his colleagues had tried to convince him to reconsider, but he'd been adamant about pulling up stakes and they'd finally accepted his decision. A week later they'd found a replacement, who'd stepped into his shoes without the smallest hiccup, and life went on.

It would for Ivy Harris, too. Besides, she'd seemed resourceful enough to locate someone to do what he could not.

But what if she didn't?

She'd manage. Managing was what doctors did best, especially under the most difficult of circumstances.

You don't have any children, do you, Dr. Locke?

Ivy's voice echoed in his head and he steeled himself against the pain. She'd definitely played hardball with her remark, but he hadn't been inclined to explain how every one of his tiny, tiny patients had been "his" kid. And he certainly hadn't been about to admit that he'd fathered one of his own, because it would have prompted an entirely new set of questions; questions that would only lead to him reliving what still lay so heavily on his heart.

In spite of his expertise, in spite of the advances in modern medicine, he hadn't been able to save his own son.

"How long has Robbie had this patch on his arm?" she asked Molly Owens.

Molly shrugged. "Several weeks. At first I thought it was just part of his allergies, so I used an over-the-counter cortisone cream. But the area is getting larger, so I thought it was time to try something else." The thirty-year-old grinned. "Unless you're going to tell me I haven't given the cream enough time to work?"

The lesion was about the size of a silver dollar, red and flat, and the center was scaly looking. A textbook picture if she ever saw one.

"Not a chance," Ivy said with a smile. "Your cream won't help. Robbie has ringworm. It's a fungus infection and requires special medication."

"Ringworm?" Molly was aghast. "Are you sure?"

"I could do a skin scraping for fungus and send it to the lab, if you'd like, but I'm certain about my diagnosis."

"Oh, I'm not questioning you," Molly was quick to reply. "It's just that I thought it was transmitted from animals, and we don't have a dog or a cat."

"That's often the case," Ivy agreed, "but sometimes a child will pick up the fungus from the soil."

Molly exhaled a long-suffering sigh. "He does love to play in the dirt with his trucks," she said as she fingercombed the little boy's sandy-colored hair.

"See my truck?" Robbie held the metal vehicle under Ivy's nose. "It goes fast. Vroooom, *vroooom.*"

"I see," Ivy told him. "I'll bet you're an excellent driver."

Focused on his toy, and making the appropriate engine noises, Robbie jumped off his mom's lap and began pushing it along the linoleum.

"So what do I do?" Molly asked. "Keep him out of the dirt?"

"You can try, but I suspect you'll fight a losing battle."

"To put it mildly."

Ivy wrote on her prescription pad. "Here's a script for an anti-fungal cream. Apply it to his arm twice daily."

"For how long?"

"Until the patch disappears, which will take a few weeks."

"That's it?"

"You should also sterilize his towels, his bedding, and any clothes that come in contact with the area. You don't want this to spread to anyone else in your family."

"OK. Not a problem."

"If you notice the lesion becomes redder, or oozes pus, come back. Same for if it hasn't disappeared in three or four weeks. And if by some chance you notice another area developing, start treating it immediately with the cream."

"Will do. Thanks so much, Doctor."

Ivy smiled as she escorted Molly to the door of the exam room. "You're welcome."

Heather waited outside the cubicle. "You aren't going to believe this—"

"After today, I can believe anything," Ivy said dryly. "How many more patients are waiting?"

"None." The woman grinned. "Robbie was the last one."

Ivy glanced at the clock. 6:15 p.m. "You're right. I don't believe it. I thought we'd be here until seven at least."

"Same here. I guess we were lucky. And, speaking of lucky, you have a visitor."

It was too late in the evening for a drug rep to drop in and peddle his wares. "Who is it?"

"I have no idea. He wouldn't leave his name, but he's quite a hunk if you ask me."

"Then it's no one you know?"

"Nope, which is a shame. He's the sort who would have women flocking around him if he'd bother to smile. He's the dark, brooding Heathcliffe type."

Instantly a picture of Ethan Locke flashed into Ivy's head, but she dismissed the idea. He wouldn't have any reason to stop by her office. No doubt he'd rather walk barefoot through a Texas sandburr patch than run into her again.

"OK, I'll find out who he is and what he wants. Meanwhile, enjoy your evening at home."

"I will."

Ivy told her receptionist goodnight, then beelined to the waiting room. "Sorry to keep you waiting," she told the tall fellow who was studying one of her favorite Anne Geddes prints, depicting three babies decked out in yellow bunny costumes, spooning each other as they lay fast asleep.

He turned to face her and she caught her breath.

Ethan Locke.

He didn't look much different than he had earlier, although he'd shaved, revealing an endearing dimple in his chin.

"Well, well, this is a surprise," she said evenly, both suspicious and curious as to why he'd tracked her down. But she didn't intend to make it easy for him. "If you want a refill on your antisocial pills you'll have to see Jed, because I don't treat adults. His office is next door."

His face turned ruddy. "I deserve that, I suppose, but I came to apologize."

He'd surprised her, because on the basis of their first meeting she hadn't thought he was the sort to worry over what she or anyone else might think of him, much less apologize for his actions. If she weren't so tired, and if she didn't have hospital rounds to make yet, she might have been willing to spar with him for a while longer. But she was, and she did, and she wanted to fall into bed as soon as possible.

"Accepted. Now, if you'll excuse me—"

"Wait."

The one word stopped her in her tracks. She studied him carefully, noticing how he seemed to hesitate, as if he needed to bolster his courage. Instinctively, she knew his apology was only an excuse. Perhaps even a test of some sort….

"Look," she said slowly, "I'd love to stay and chat, but I have a hundred and one things to do before this day officially ends. If you're here for a reason, just spit it out and save me the suspense. I don't have the energy to play twenty questions."

"Have you found someone to help you?"

"I haven't had time," she admitted. "But, as you said, I'm sure I'll find someone. Eventually. Why do you ask?"

She'd wanted to say *Why do you care?,* but she'd eaten lunch, and they'd finished earlier than she'd expected, so she could afford to be nice. For the moment.

He paused, his gaze steady. "Because I'm offering my services."

CHAPTER TWO

FROM the expression on Ivy's face, Ethan had obviously startled her speechless. He wouldn't blame her if she told him to buzz off, after they'd parted on less than friendly terms. Part of him hoped she wouldn't, but if she did he would go back to his rented cabin with his conscience appeased.

Her surprise disappeared and her face settled into more impassive lines, as if she wanted to believe but wouldn't allow herself to do so. "You're offering to help?"

"Yes."

"If this is some twisted idea of a joke…"

"It isn't. It's a sincere offer."

"Forgive me, but I'd never dreamed… You're actually willing to help me." She narrowed her coffee-colored eyes in obvious suspicion as she dug her hands into her white lab coat.

"For a few weeks." He'd thought about extending on open-ended offer without a set final date as he planned to live in the area until the end of the summer, but he wanted—no, *needed* an escape clause. Helping a colleague in dire straits for a few weeks should be enough to appease his conscience.

"Several hours ago you said you weren't interested. What prompted you to change your mind?"

"Does it matter?" he countered, unwilling to explain how, after her you-don't-have-children comment, his former colleague and old friend's phone call had tipped the scales in her favor.

"*Try something different,*" Stewart Trimble had urged. "*I understand your reasons for steering clear of medicine, but you still have a lot to give.*"

"*I don't,*" Ethan had replied flatly. "*The proverbial well is dry.*"

"*Temporarily, perhaps, but you aren't a quitter, Ethan,*" Stewart had said. "*Pediatricians aren't limited to treating infants, you know. After bumming around the country for the last six months, don't you owe yourself the old college try? What would it hurt to agree to a locum job in a practice where the worst thing you'll treat is a sore throat and an occasional cough? Maybe your well isn't as dry as you think.*"

Plenty, he'd wanted to say, but in the end the combination of seeing Ivy's exhaustion, the new load of guilt she'd leveled on him, and Stewart's thought-provoking encouragement had prompted him to drive into town and offer his services on a limited scale for an equally limited amount of time. It would be a trial period, he'd consoled himself as the distance to Ivy's clinic had shortened. That was all. At the end of the three weeks she'd asked for he'd have a better idea of what he'd do with the rest of his life.

As an added bonus, perhaps he could get the attractive Ivy Harris out of his head. His fiancée had been every bit as beautiful, but he'd soon learned that beauty usually only went skin deep.

She cleared her throat, bringing him back to the present. "No," she admitted. "Although I want to be sure you won't fill in for a day and quit the next because you changed your mind."

"I finish what I start. If I agree to help you for three weeks, then I won't leave you high and dry." His former colleagues at the children's hospital could attest to that. Once he'd tendered his resignation in St. Louis, he could have walked away, but through sheer force of will he'd struggled through another month until a replacement could be found.

She fell silent, apparently digesting his information. "OK. When can you start?"

"Whenever you like."

She laughed, the lighthearted sound easing the residual tightness in his chest that hadn't left him since the day his son had died. "I'd say immediately, but tomorrow is soon enough."

"Tomorrow it is," he said. "But I have a few conditions."

A long-suffering expression flitted across her face, as if she half expected him to list requirements she couldn't possibly meet. "Something tells me I need to sit down to hear this," she said wryly as she did exactly that. "OK. Give me your terms."

"First of all, I'll earn the same salary you do and pay the same expenses."

She blinked twice owlishly, as if he'd surprised her—which he probably had. "That isn't what I initially offered you."

"As I said earlier, I don't take advantage of a colleague. Especially one who's starting out."

"Thanks." She sounded dubious, as if she were afraid he'd spring something worse on her.

He did. "Second, I won't treat babies."

"None at all?"

"Infants aren't my forte," he said flatly. "I'll take on all the school-age kids and adolescents who walk through the door, but anyone under the age of three is yours to deal with."

She opened her mouth as if to argue, then simply nodded, as if she'd decided she could live with that particular stipulation. In a town without obstetrical services there couldn't be more babies, especially newborns, than she could handle on her own.

"OK," she said calmly. "Anything else?"

"Isn't that enough?"

Her face warmed. "I'd say so. But at this point I can't afford to be choosy. I appreciate anything and everything you're willing to do." She rose. "I'm usually here by seven-thirty most mornings, and our first patients are scheduled for nine."

"What about referrals?"

"I send any child who needs a specialist north to Wichita or south to Oklahoma City," she continued, "depending on the parents' preference and insurance requirements. My goal is to bring in a pediatric endocrinologist and allergist once a month for scheduled appointments, but with everything that's happened I haven't had a chance to organize the clinics. Walt and I have other plans we hope to implement, but, as they say, Rome wasn't built in a day." Her smile was rueful.

Ethan saw the enthusiasm, the confidence, the full-steam-ahead attitude he'd seen in every new board-certified physician. Faith in one's skills and the miracles of modern medicine made a man, or a woman, feel invincible and ready to conquer the world. For an instant he wanted to advise her to enjoy that feeling, because she'd lose it soon enough.

Idly, he wondered if he'd made a huge mistake by coming here. Seeing Ivy Harris every day would be like looking in a mirror, reminding him of what he'd once been like and showing him what he was now. A jaded physician didn't pair well with an eager, idealistic one, but he'd already committed himself and he couldn't back out now. Not because he cared about Ivy's opinion, but because keeping his word was a matter of family honor. He might be the only Locke left, but his personal integrity was something he intended to hold on to with both hands.

"In the meantime," Ivy continued, "if you have a patient who needs a referral, check with Heather, my nurse, or Billie, our receptionist."

"You only have one nurse?"

"At the moment. But don't worry. I'll find another RN. They aren't as difficult to come by as doctors," she tacked on wryly. "If you'd like, I can show you around now, or we can wait until morning."

"Don't you have a hundred and one things to do before you can call it a day?" He turned her own words against her, although he found himself unwilling to leave for reasons he didn't quite understand.

She smiled tiredly. "Yeah, but it won't take long to give the nickel tour. We can start—" Her cellphone rang and she glanced at the caller ID display. "This might take a few minutes. Feel free to wander around on your own."

Ethan sauntered past the receptionist's desk as he ignored Ivy's one-sided conversation. He stepped into the first patient room and saw the required glass canisters of cotton balls, cotton-tipped applicator sticks and tongue depressors standing on the counter, next to an otoscope to look into the ear canal. A biohazard container for needles and syringes hung on the wall.

Inside the cabinets and drawers he found the odd assortment of other necessities, including facial tissues, blood pressure cuffs in different sizes for little arms, as well as various kits and irrigation solutions. As far as he could tell Ivy had stocked her office with everything a general pediatrician might need, probably to avoid sending her patients on a lengthy drive elsewhere.

He sensed Ivy's presence at the door before she uttered a word. Turning, he saw the slight frown on her face.

"Problems?" he asked.

She nodded. "I have to go. There's been an accident. A truck collided with a van carrying six children, ages nine months to eight years old."

It would be daunting to treat that many cases at once, especially if those six were critical. Clearly Jed wouldn't be much help, because he'd have his hands full with the adults involved.

All afternoon he'd convinced himself he'd do nothing more than swab sore throats, peer into achy ears and listen to a few asthmatic lungs. Unfortunately fate had thrown another curve ball at him. No doubt Stewart would laugh his fool head off if he knew the situation Ethan had landed in without warning.

She waited silently, but he saw the unspoken plea in her eyes. The way he saw it, he had three options. He could ignore her silent request and simply say goodbye—an option which appealed mightily because he technically wasn't on duty until tomorrow; he could do nothing—in which case she'd probably beg; or he could put his plans for dinner and a quiet evening at home aside and volunteer.

Some choices. Two would make him a heartless jerk and one would ruin the rest of his already ruined day. Having decided to fill in out of guilt, he might as well get started, he decided reluctantly, although it had been a while since he'd used his general pediatric skills. Still, he had an advantage: unlike the pre-term neonates he'd treated, the children he'd work with now could point him in the right direction.

"Would you like me to assist?" he asked, hoping she'd refuse.

She positively beamed, and took a step forward. For a moment she wore such a supreme look of relief that he thought she might kiss him.

He wouldn't have minded. In fact, just the possibility of feeling her lips against his sent blood rushing through his body. *Geesh*, having such a strong physical reaction on the basis of merely *thinking* about a kiss plainly indicated he'd been alone for too long.

Yet, physical attraction or not, he didn't have any business letting his imagination run away from him. He carried too much emotional baggage right now to consider any sort of relationship, even a platonic one.

Instead of kissing him, as he'd both feared and anticipated, she grabbed his hand and squeezed gently. "Oh, thank you. I'd love it if you would. Mind you, if it's all minor stuff you can leave, but it would be great to have you nearby. Just in case things get complicated."

It already was, he thought wryly, deciding her touch could easily become addictive. She was warm and vibrant, in a world which had been cold and colorless, but rather than allow himself the luxury of enjoying it to the fullest he mentally distanced himself at the same time as he abruptly extricated his hand from hers. Emotionally entangling himself with a pretty woman who'd want more from him than he could possibly give was a prescription for more heartache. He'd seen the light in one woman's eyes fade into accusation and disgust. He wasn't about to experience that again.

"Then shall we go?" he asked, his voice impersonal.

Her face turned a rosy hue, as if she recognized his brush-off. "Yes," she said, her tone several degrees chillier than it had been before. "We should."

As he followed her down the hallway that connected their clinic to the hospital, he noticed her demeanor toward him had turned from warm-hearted to strictly professional. Yet when she called a fellow named Ted she went back to being congenial and bubbly again. Clearly she'd chosen to save her friendly overtures for someone who wanted them, which was perfectly fine with him.

Yes, it was best for everyone concerned if they kept their relationship on a businesslike footing during the few weeks they were together. But, while it was the logical thing to do, he couldn't deny the sense of loss that swept through him.

With one phone call to Ted Burns, the hospital's CEO, Ivy had gotten Ethan consultant status so he could begin treating patients.

"It's all set," she said, as soon as she'd slipped her cell-phone into her pocket. "You have temporary privileges with final approval contingent on you coming in tomorrow to show your credentials and sign the necessary paperwork."

"So soon? I'm impressed."

His surprise grated on her nerves. It was as if he hadn't expected anyone in town to be efficient. "We don't all work at Lew's speeds of slow and slower yet," she said smartly.

He raised an eyebrow. "I'm glad to hear it."

No, she decided with some disappointment, Ethan Locke wouldn't win the Friendliest Doctor of the Year award. Wariest, perhaps, or Gruffest, or Most Reluctant, or even Most Mysterious—but Friendliest? Not a chance.

But what did it matter if he frowned all day long, never spoke more than a few words and kept to himself? As long as he was kind to the patients and proved himself competent she would be one happy doctor.

Yet, regardless of how she'd characterized him, she also knew that people were a product of their experiences. What had made Ethan Locke so determined to isolate himself?

Whatever his reasons, she could either respond in kind or treat him as she did everyone else. The choice was easy to the point that it wasn't a choice at all.

She bestowed one of her usual smiles on him as she led the way toward a cart near the ambulance bay that held protective gear. "We're not as hung up on bureaucracy as other places, and we're more flexible, but don't forget to see Ted first thing in the morning. He'll bend what can be bent, but only so far."

"See Ted first. Got it."

As Ivy shrugged on the familiar yellow gown, vinyl gloves and face shield, she noticed Ethan doing the same. "We'll wait out—"

Nancy Martinez, the middle-aged nurse who was in charge of the department, approached at a near-run. "I just heard. ETA of the ambulance is three minutes. We're getting the Ellerbe twins."

Ivy's heart sank. The twins were nine months old and their parents' pride and joy. "Marybeth?"

"She was driving," Nancy said, her forehead furrowed with concern. "Apparently she'd taken the kids in her daycare to Wichita Zoo today, and was coming home when a truck ran a stop sign and plowed into her. Luckily she'd already delivered several of the kids at their homes before it happened, otherwise we'd have three more patients."

"I assume you know the family?" Ethan asked.

"I grew up with Marybeth's husband and I know his mother quite well. By the way, Ethan, this is Nancy, our E.R. charge nurse. She's worked here for years, and knows everything there is to know about the hospital. So if there's anything you need, she's your go-to person." She turned to Nancy. "This is Dr. Ethan Locke. He's helping us out temporarily."

An ambulance siren wailed in the distance. "Come on," she said. "We're being paged."

The heat, coupled with her protective gear, blasted her after being in the air-conditioned facility. Almost immediately a host of other staff members materialized to surround them.

"Everybody!" Ivy called out to the assembled group as the ambulance approached the loading dock. "This is Dr. Ethan

Locke, and he will be helping us for the next few weeks. He's a pediatrician and he comes highly recommended."

Actually, she didn't have any recommendations about him at all, other than Lew's observation that he'd been a physician at the prestigious children's hospital in St. Louis. He could be a doctor who couldn't hack the job, but her instincts said that wasn't the case. He had too much intelligence shining out of his eyes that no amount of cynicism and rudeness could disguise. Her biggest consolation lay in Nancy, who knew her stuff and would alert Ivy if his decisions were questionable.

Having done all she could to stack the odds in the victims' favor, she riveted her attention on the emergency vehicle. Even with the back doors closed she heard the babies' cries.

She glanced at Ethan, and was surprised by his stone-faced demeanor and grim expression, but she couldn't ponder the reasons for it now.

Before the vehicle edged to a complete stop, she drew a bracing breath and yanked open the doors. Inside were two babies strapped into their infant seats, kicking and screaming in stereo, two older children—girls about five and six—who were doing their best to console the inconsolable babies, and a sandy-haired boy about seven years old, strapped to a backboard and sporting a c-spine collar, an IV line, a mask and a tank of oxygen between his legs.

"Packed house," Ivy commented to the paramedic over the frightened wail of the babies. "What do you have?"

"One with abdominal injuries and four ambulatory—if you consider a car seat being ambulatory," Ben Kovacs, the paramedic, reported. "I gave those two a preliminary once-over." He motioned to the little noise-makers. "From their volume, I think they're more scared than hurt, so I left them in their car seats for easy transport."

"Crying is good. I'd be more worried if they weren't making a sound." Ethan had stationed himself near the boy's gurney, but Ivy knew they couldn't move the stretcher until the littlest ones were out of the way. Ben had truly packed the victims inside.

"They've only stopped long enough to take a breath and catch their second wind," Ben said wryly. "I figured you could check them out more thoroughly to make sure they were OK."

Ivy handed one carrier to Ethan before she reached for the other, noticing the huge tears clinging to soggy eyelashes, the red screwed-up faces and runny noses. By the time she'd handed the other infant to waiting nurses Ethan had already passed his bundle to someone else. He'd obviously hadn't taken time to give the baby more than a passing glance, if that.

"Put them in Room One and I'll be there in a minute," Ivy directed, and she waved the older girls forward out of the corner where Ben had squeezed them.

"Suzy and Emma only have bumps and bruises," Ben reported, his attention focused on the boy in front of him. "They could have waited, but I thought they should get away from the scene as soon as possible. Some things a kid shouldn't see," he finished in a low voice.

Ivy's imagination filled in the blanks. "Come on, girls. Let's go where I can make sure you're okay, too." Grabbing their hands, she helped them hop off the back bumper into the care of a young certified nurses' aide, Robyn.

With the extraneous people out of the way, Ben released the latch holding the gurney in place. Between the three of them they pulled the stretcher out of the emergency vehicle and snapped the wheels in place before rolling their patient inside. Through it all, Ben gave his report.

"Tommy, here, is the worst. He was sitting behind the driver on the same side of the van where the truck plowed into them. BP is low, pulse is rapid." Ben rattled off the numbers.

"I'll look after him," Ethan told Ivy as he helped guide the gurney into the trauma room. "You take care of the rest."

Ivy hesitated. "Are you sure?"

"You're the one in charge of babies," he reminded her.

"OK." Yet she found herself unable to leave. Not because she didn't trust him—OK, maybe she had a few doubts—but mainly because she felt as if she were throwing him to the wolves by asking him to handle a trauma in a place where he'd never stepped foot until now.

For the first time since she'd accepted his offer she wondered if she'd made the right decision to bring in a relative unknown.

"Do you know how old he is?" she heard Ethan ask Ben.

"He's seven."

One advantage to a small community was that everyone knew everyone, which worked out nicely during times like these. Someday she'd know everyone in town by sight, too, but she'd been gone for years and hadn't been back nearly long enough to have that ability today.

Ethan leaned over the moving gurney as he lightly gripped the boy's hand. "Hi, Tommy. I'm Ethan, and we're going to make you feel better soon."

He sniffled. "I want…my mommy," he sobbed.

"I know," Ethan soothed. "We're going to get your parents here as soon as we can. Can you tell me where you hurt?"

One hand fluttered to his abdomen. "Stomach. My chest."

They rolled the gurney into the trauma room, and an instant later they'd moved Tommy, still strapped to the backboard with his head immobilized, to a hospital bed.

"Just hang on a little bit longer while we run some tests and take a few pictures," Ethan told the youngster kindly. "Can you do that for me, sport?"

Tommy's lower lip trembled. "I'll…I'll try."

Ethan stroked a wayward lock of hair out of Tommy's eyes. "Fair enough."

Ivy had been afraid Ethan didn't have a compassionate cell in his body, but his simple, kindly actions blasted away her lingering doubts. He might be gruff, but he cared about his patients.

What in the world was he doing in Danton? Even if he wanted an extended vacation, she would have guessed a more exotic, touristy place would have been his choice.

"If you don't need me anymore, Doc," Ben said to Ethan, "I gotta go back. They were using the Jaws of Life to extricate the driver of the van when we left, and because they aren't back yet…"

"Marybeth?"

Ben looked surprised. "Do you know her?"

"Only what Nancy told us before you arrived. And if Nancy says we can manage on our own, then we'll see you later."

The nurse looked surprised, but pleased he'd consulted her. "We'll be OK. See you later, Ben."

"Thanks for your help," Ethan seconded, before he addressed Nancy. "Start another IV, large bore needle with lactated Ringer's."

An instant later he patted the boy's hand and began examining his abdomen and chest. Suddenly he cocked his head and frowned, as if he'd heard something he didn't like.

Ivy listened, too, and recognized the distinctive wail of babies—the same noise she'd blocked out earlier.

"Still here, Dr. Harris?" Ethan mentioned idly.

Caught in the act! But it had been worth it, because she'd seen enough to rest easier in the abilities of her temporary partner. "I'm leaving now," she promised, doing just that.

Yet as she examined the twins, ordered a few precautionary X-rays and lab tests, as well as a bottle of formula for each, she found herself impatient to return.

Funny thing how Ethan's training and previous experience as a general pediatrician seemed to surface from out of nowhere as he examined his young patient. Apparently it was true that some things, like riding a bike, just weren't forgotten, because from the moment Ethan saw the bruises on Tommy's torso, the abdominal rigidity, cool clammy skin and shocky vital signs, he knew what to do. Grateful that he wasn't in over his head as much as he'd feared, he relaxed a bit and mentally ran through the diagnostic protocol.

"I want cervical and lumbar spine X-rays, as well as chest and abdominal films," he told Nancy, guessing that the two people lingering in the background were the lab and X-ray techs. "A CBC, basic chemistries, liver enzymes, renal function, amylase, type and cross-match for two units, coag studies, and a urinalysis. Stat. Any chance we can get a CT scan?"

Nancy shook her head. "Sorry. We've been trying to raise money for a scanner, but haven't yet."

The scan would have ruled out intra-abdominal or peritoneal bleeding, but if one wasn't available then he'd have to depend on other tests to make his diagnosis. For the first time since he'd left St. Louis he realized how fortunate he'd been to have every resource available.

He stepped aside to allow the techs to work, remaining nearby to watch Tommy's monitors, guess at his weight and double-check his mental calculations for the amount of fluid replacement.

By the time Ivy rematerialized he'd run a nasogastric tube and ruled out a stomach injury, gotten a baseline hemoglobin level from the lab, studied the films and decided the spine immobilization could be discontinued—although he'd feel better if a radiologist had given his seal of approval.

"Reinforcements have arrived," she said cheerfully. "What can I do?"

"Find a surgeon in the next thirty minutes."

"I wish. What's the problem? Internal bleeding?"

Ethan pulled her aside. "I think his spleen's ruptured. I don't have a second hemoglobin level yet, but he has all the signs, especially abdominal pain and tenderness, pain in his left shoulder, and being shocky. The question is, do you want to observe him here and then Medevac him out when we know for certain, or move him close to an O.R. now, before he needs one?"

"Do you really have to ask?" Her tone was wry.

"I'd vote to move him out now, but this is my first day on the job," he reminded her. "I'm still learning your protocol."

"The only protocol I have is that I make a point never to gamble with my patients' lives. I'd rather give them an unnecessary helicopter ride than hold them here until it's too late." She met his gaze. "Do you have a problem with that?"

"Not at all," he admitted. "I'd hoped you'd agree with me."

"Then I'll make the arrangements."

"As an FYI," Ethan mentioned before Ivy got too far, "Ben said they were using the Jaws of Life to free this Marybeth person, so she might need to catch a chopper ride, too."

"I'll notify the air dispatch."

After making the flight arrangements, Ivy ran into Jed outside the trauma room. The same age as Walt, Jed was looking as haggard as Ivy felt.

"Busy day for you, too?" she commiserated.

He smiled. "I haven't worked this hard in years. How Walt did it all by himself is a mystery. Not to mention downright miraculous."

Ivy chuckled. "I have to agree."

The ambulance bay doors whooshed open and the E.M.T. crew wheeled in another victim. At the same time the main doors at the other end of the department flew open, and a crowd of frantic adults rushed through.

"Have fun with that group," Jed murmured, before he sprinted toward the incoming gurney and disappeared inside the trauma room where Ethan and Tommy already were.

Immediately Ivy was surrounded by parents asking after their children. After trying unsuccessfully to get a word in edgewise, she gave an unladylike whistle.

Complete and utter silence followed.

"Who belongs with Suzy and/or Emma?"

A young couple and a single woman raised their hands.

"Tommy?"

"He's our son," another couple said.

Ivy smiled. "Dr. Ethan is with him right now, but I'll let him know you're here. The rest of you—" she glanced at the other parents "—come with me."

She led her group to a nearby treatment room, where she paused in the hall. "Both Suzy and Emma are fine," she told them. "They have some bruises and bumps, and will be sore for a couple of days, but nothing that a few hot baths and plenty of rest won't cure."

"Are you sure?" The woman who'd identified herself as Emma's mother asked.

"Absolutely. But if they complain about anything new in the next couple of days, be sure you bring them in. In the meantime they can have acetaminophen to ease their aches and pains."

"Thanks, Dr. Ivy." Suzy's father pumped her hand. "We appreciate this."

"Can we take our girls home now?" Emma's mother asked.

"Absolutely." Ivy opened the door and the two girls inside

jumped up and ran to their parents. Amid hugs and tears and sniffles, the two chattered like a pair of blue jays as they described the accident.

Happy to send those two on their way, Ivy peeked into the room where the twins slept in the baby beds that someone had robbed from the medical ward, clearly worn out from their experience.

Determined to let Ethan handle the other set of waiting parents, she found him next to Tommy's bed. "How's he doing?" she asked, ignoring Jed and the nurses surrounding his patient for the moment.

"Stable, for the moment. His second hemoglobin level has dropped, though."

"ETA for the helicopter, twenty minutes. Which was at least…" she checked her watch "…seven minutes ago."

"Good."

"His parents are waiting outside. I thought you should talk to them as you know his condition better than I do."

He hesitated, as if hating to leave Tommy's side.

"I'll stay," Nancy offered. "His vital signs haven't changed in the last fifteen minutes. I'll let you know if they do."

Ivy accompanied Ethan to the nurses' station, where the Weathers were still waiting. From the worry on their faces, they obviously expected to hear the worst.

"How is Tommy?" his father asked. "Can we see him?"

"In just a minute," Ethan said, before he introduced himself. "Tommy's suffered abdominal trauma and I believe he has a ruptured spleen."

At Mrs. Weathers's gasp, he continued, "He's stable for the moment, but he's going to need surgery and soon."

"How soon?"

"Within hours, I'd say," Ethan admitted. "Dr. Harris has called for an air ambulance. It should be here any minute now to fly him to Wichita, where a surgeon is already waiting for him."

"Is that the only thing wrong?" Mrs. Weathers's voice and mouth trembled. "His spleen?"

"As far as I can tell. His X-rays didn't show any problems with his spine, although we'll have a radiologist read them to be absolutely certain. He can also wiggle his fingers and toes, so I think it's safe to say he'll be running around before long. As for other conditions—his liver and kidney function tests all look good, but the surgeon will know more after he takes a look inside. Afterward they'll continue to monitor him closely. Sometimes problems crop up a day or two after the accident. For now, the immediate problem is to stop the internal bleeding."

"Won't it stop on its own?" Mr. Weathers asked.

"The spleen is a highly vascular organ, which means it's full of blood vessels. Its function is to filter all the blood as it enters the circulation. The only way to stop Tommy's bleeding is to remove the organ."

His parents' faces blanched. "If his spleen is a filter, won't he need it?"

"As important as it is," Ethan explained, "one can live without it."

"Can we see him, Doctor?"

"For a few minutes—until the air crew gets here. Don't worry, they'll send a nurse and an E.M.T., so Tommy will have excellent care while he's flying. Mind you, though, when you see him he'll be groggy, and may not make much sense," he warned. "And don't be alarmed by the tubes and monitors." He smiled. "Your son has been a real trooper. He's a tough little character."

Throughout Ethan's conversation Ivy had hung in the background. She gave him high marks for his bedside manner.

Once again she wondered why a physician of his apparent caliber had been so reluctant to answer her first call for help. She was equally curious as to why he'd changed his mind. But, whatever his reasons, she was glad that he had. Considering how Tommy was the only one who'd been critically injured, she probably could have managed on her own while Walt's nurse practitioner dealt with the twins and the two older girls. However, it was nice having another physician available. As Jed had said, it was nothing short of miraculous how Walt had managed singlehandedly.

Idly, she wondered if she could talk Ethan into sticking around to help them as long as he remained in the area. It certainly wouldn't hurt to ask, or at least to plant that seed of an idea and see what germinated. After all, what did she have to lose?

CHAPTER THREE

ALTHOUGH Tommy's case was textbook, and Ethan didn't harbor any doubts about his treatment decisions, he didn't breathe easier until the flight crew arrived and hauled the seven-year-old away with conscientious precision. So much *could* have gone wrong, and without a local surgeon to intervene, the consequences could have been dire.

To his relief, everything had run smoothly, and by the time his part in tonight's drama had ended, pride and a sense of accomplishment that he hadn't experienced in a long time stirred inside of him. A shrink would probably psychoanalyze his response and suggest some nonsense about how it signaled he was ready to return to medicine full-time, but Ethan didn't believe in signs or hidden meanings. Wearing a stethoscope again was due to a fluke, not a conscious decision to return to the profession he'd walked away from without a backward glance. No, he was here in Danton's hospital because he was simply trying to prevent another load of guilt from settling on his overburdened shoulders.

Surprisingly enough, though, for a few hours his first foray back into medicine had held his personal demons at bay, but he knew better than to believe they would be gone forever. After his son had died, he'd carried on as usual, believing that long hours and hard work were the best way to cope with his grief and feelings of inadequacy.

He'd been wrong. His relief had come when he'd walked out of the neonatal ICU for the last time.

Demons or not, though, he had to admit the Danton hospital staff's efficiency in assembling all of Tommy's X-rays, lab reports, and the temperature-controlled box containing extra units of cross-matched blood were impressive. Shipping critically ill patients might be a routine situation for them, but, routine or not, the staff had been as organized as any he'd seen in a major hospital.

They'd done the same less than hour later, when another helicopter had arrived to take Marybeth Ellerbe.

He planned to comment to Ivy about the group's performance, but when she appeared with one of the twins tucked against her shoulder, his good intentions fled as he concentrated on ignoring the baby.

"How did it go?" he asked, referring to her conversation with Marybeth Ellerbe's husband, Allen.

"He's numb," she admitted. "I'm not certain anything we said soaked in. After Jed and I told him we'd sent her on because of a dislocated hip, broken femur and perforated lung, he got this dazed look in his eyes."

"He surely knows he needs to pull himself together for his daughters' sake?"

"Barely," she said on a sigh. "For a minute there I wondered if he even remembered he had twins, but he finally phoned his mother. She's on her way to get them as we speak."

He glanced around. "So where is he?"

She rubbed the baby's back. "He's on his way to Wichita. I only hope he doesn't do something stupid, like try to break speed records." She paused. "Still charting?"

"Just finishing." He scrawled his name, then tucked the pen in the pencil cup with the others. "What about you?"

"Mine's done, too. Or it will be as soon as I discharge the twins into their grandmother's care." She swayed a little to rock the baby. "Thanks again for helping out. Things went rather well, if I say so myself. We stabilized both of our critical patients and no one died. I still can't believe the guy in the truck walked away without a scratch."

"It happens more often than not." He leaned back in his chair and stretched to ease the ache between his shoulder blades. "I wish we would have had a surgeon on staff, though."

"Someday we will. Walt's been working on bringing in more doctors for years. He's got a lead on a young internist who's interested in getting away from the city to raise his family, and he's actively looking for an OB-GYN to either move here or at least establish prenatal clinics. If all goes well, before long we'll be able to deliver more than basic medical care."

"Optimistic, are you?"

She laughed. "I am, so I'll take that as a compliment." She turned slightly away from him. "Is she asleep?" she whispered.

He had no choice but to look, to notice the downy-soft skin, the rosebud mouth, and the little fingers that were just large enough to wrap trustingly around a finger. This little one seemed like a giant when he compared her to the two-pound neonates he'd once held in the palm of one hand, but it wasn't the size that got to him. It was the helplessness and the inherent trust they placed in the ones who cared for them.

And he'd failed.

"Yes," he said shortly.

"Good. Her sister is already asleep, but Tory has been fighting it. Isn't she the sweetest thing?" Ivy cooed.

"Yeah, sure." Desperate to escape before she suggested he do something inconceivable, like hold the baby, he rose. "If you don't mind, I'm going to call it a day."

"Good idea. I'll see you tomorrow morning at eight?"

She'd stated it as a question, as if she were afraid he'd suffered a change of heart. "Afraid I won't show up?" he asked.

Her face matched the pink blanket covering the baby. "The thought crossed my mind." She sounded defensive.

He couldn't fault her for worrying. Ivy didn't know him well enough to have any faith in him, and it was probably a good thing she didn't. Otherwise she'd know she shouldn't trust a man who'd given up medicine some six months and six hundred miles ago.

"I'll be there," he said gruffly.

To Ivy's surprise, she saw Ethan much sooner than she'd expected.

After placing the twins into the care of their grandmother, Barbara Ellerbe, Ivy drove to her dad's diner. The Tuesday Night Roast Beef Special might be gone, but she was hungry enough to eat some of his trademark five-alarm chili.

She pulled into the restaurant's gravel parking lot, hardly noticing that the neon sign proclaiming "Don's Diner" was missing the *R*. Instead, she noticed a late-model saloon surrounded by the well-used pickup trucks and economy cars.

There was only one person in town who might own such a pricey vehicle, and seeing Ethan Locke seated alone at a booth in the far right corner confirmed her suspicions.

Her father apparently had counter duty, because he was pouring coffee for the customers at one end, so Ivy wound her way past the occupied tables toward a free barstool at the opposite end. It took her longer than her aching feet wanted, because everyone she walked by greeted her and struck up a conversation, but she finally reached her destination and sank onto the vinyl-cushioned seat with a heartfelt sigh.

A minute later her father joined her, wearing his usual white butcher's apron which, at this time of day, was stained and spotted with everything from coffee to pie filling.

"Well, look what the cat dragged in," Don Harris teased as he grabbed a clean, white, heavy-duty ceramic mug from the rack behind him and poured it full of decaf. "I heard about the wreck."

She didn't doubt that he had. News traveled fast, and it usually filtered through the only restaurant in town. "Nothing slips by you, does it, Dad?" she teased.

He shook his head. At fifty-seven, his once-black hair was now liberally streaked with silver, and smile lines etched his face. A large-boned man, who epitomized the description of a gentle giant, his kindness and generosity to the people who walked through his business establishment matched his size.

"Not a thing," he agreed. "How are Marybeth and young Tommy?"

"They were both in serious condition when they left us. We haven't gotten any word as yet, but barring any complications, I'd say they'll both heal."

"That's good news, then. I also heard you got yourself some extra help." He nodded in Ethan's direction.

"I did," she admitted. "And I'm glad."

"I am, too, honey," he told her. "You're looking a little frayed around the edges."

"Gee, thanks, Dad," she said with a tired smile as she stirred creamer into her drink. "Nothing makes a girl happier than hearing she looks less than her best."

"Don't be silly. No one sees you like I do. As your dad, I have an advantage."

"As your daughter, I can use the same excuse. Now that

I've finished med school, when are you going to slow down? Bring someone in to run things for you?"

"Not that again," he protested. "What would I do all day if I didn't putter around here?"

"Fish, golf, travel. Relax and enjoy life."

"I *am* enjoying life just fine, without fishing, golfing and traveling."

"Then find a hobby. Surely there's something you've always wanted to do and couldn't?" Her face brightened. "You could take up woodworking again."

"And have you worry about me nailing my fingers or sawing a couple off, like your mother did? No, thanks. For the record, I'm doing what I want to do. End of story."

"But—"

"Ivy," he warned. "We've ridden this merry-go-round before. I don't work as hard as you think I do. In fact, I spend most of my day visiting with people. Nothing tiring about that."

"What about the cooking and the cleaning and the ordering, and—"

"I only work in the kitchen when Sal and Judy are gone, which isn't that often. Same for the cleaning. As for the ordering, I've done it long enough I can do it in my sleep," he boasted.

She sighed. "I suppose so."

"If you think about it, dealing with the public for the last thirty years has been my hobby. People don't just stop in here for the food," he pointed out. "A listening ear is sometimes all a fellow needs with his cup of coffee."

Ivy knew her father had heard enough stories to rival a priest's confessional, and, like a man of the cloth, he kept those tales to himself.

"I've learned to read a person's character as easily as I read the evening newspaper," he said matter-of-factly. "I wouldn't have survived in this business for as long as I have if I couldn't."

Thinking of all the people her father had quietly loaned money to in order to give them a helping hand, not to mention those who'd been so down-and-out they couldn't pay for their next meal, Ivy knew he was right. While a few people had reneged on their repayment promises, nearly everyone her dad had helped had paid him back, with interest. More importantly, the goodwill he'd created had been priceless.

"OK," she said. "I'll drop the subject."

"Thank you."

"For now," she warned. "But, because you're such an expert at reading people, tell me about Ethan Locke."

"Don't you know the man you hired to help you?"

She glanced in Ethan's direction and studied him covertly. He held his coffee mug with both hands and wore a distinct frown on his face. "At this point the only criteria I have is that he possesses a medical diploma, which checked out when I did an Internet search on him." She'd gone to the Web site for the Missouri Division of Professional Registration and had found Ethan listed as a St. Louis Children's Hospital pediatrician, which had been enough to satisfy her.

Suddenly she saw his gaze follow a young couple and their one-year-old baby as they left their nearby booth. For an instant she saw a painful yearning in his expression that took her by surprise. Quite by accident their gazes met, and she recognized the shadows in those dark depths before he glanced down at his menu.

Stunned by what she'd seen, and embarrassed because she'd obviously seen something no one was supposed to see, she turned away to give herself a chance to recover and revise her conclusions about her temporary partner.

In the space of a heartbeat she understood why he avoided people—why he was gruff and unfriendly. He was a man who was suffering and he wanted to lick his wounds in private. Whatever had brought those shadows to his eyes had claimed his spirit.

"Well," Don said slowly, "he's not the most talkative man I've run across. Keeps to himself, mainly. He tips well, which makes my waitresses happy, eats whatever is put in front of him without complaining, and pays with a credit card."

Ivy brushed aside her father's comments. She wasn't interested in Ethan's financial methods or how well he tipped the help. "I want to know about *him*—if he has a family or friends, why he chose to stop in Danton. That sort of thing."

"Ask him. If I want to know something, I ask."

"Which is why I'm quizzing you on what you know."

He sighed. "Like I said, he's not the talkative sort. If he has friends or family I couldn't say, because I never see him using his cellphone. If you want details you'll have to go right to the source. The only thing I know for certain is that he's rented the old Beckett place through the end of September."

"Really? How interesting." As it was nearly the middle of July, she mentally calculated his vacation was lasting about three months—far longer than she would have imagined any employer would allow. Unless there were extenuating circumstances…

She paused, then glanced at her father for confirmation. "He has issues to work through, doesn't he? Serious issues."

Don nodded, his brow furrowed. "I'd say so, hon. Although I doubt if anyone other than the two of us realize it. Most people don't look past his unfriendly nature to see the hurt underneath."

Ivy agreed. Ethan's self-imposed isolation clearly suggested that he didn't want his inner turmoil to be anyone's business but his own. With his "keep away" vibes no one, including herself, had dared to get close enough to learn of his internal struggles. However, now that she'd taken the time to see him from a different angle, his pain was as obvious as an elephant in the middle of a wheat field. And she'd bet a year's salary that underneath his pain was a kind, gentle man, because while he'd worked on Tommy she'd caught a glimpse of that side of him.

"I suspect being unfriendly and aloof is the way he wants it," Don continued. "A man like him has his pride. He'd hate being pitied, which is why he'd rather make everyone believe he's a rude son-of-a-gun instead of a man with problems."

"You're probably right."

Her father's expression grew troubled. "I truly hope he'll be a help to you, Ivy, but for the folks around here to accept him as someone they can count on he's going to have to meet them halfway."

She nodded. "Do you remember that collie who came around one summer? Ginger?"

"How could I forget?" he said wryly. "I had to stop you from bussing the tables before people were finished eating because you wanted plenty of scraps to give her. And heaven help them if they asked for a take-out container!"

She chuckled. "The poor thing needed to eat."

"So did my customers." The smile in his eyes contradicted the grumble in his tone.

"The point is, Dad, Ethan reminds me of Ginger. Skittish, and at times hostile. But once Ginger started to trust me, we became the best of buddies."

"Yeah, but don't forget the things you went through in the process. The worrying when she didn't show up for a few days, the rabies shots after she bit you, not to mention throwing out nearly every doll and stuffed animal you owned, including your favorite Barbie, because Ginger used them as chew toys."

"Rehabilitating her was worth every toy," she insisted.

"And you think you can do the same for him?" He tilted his head in Ethan's direction.

"I can try, Dad. I have to."

"Somehow I knew you were going to say that, but be careful you don't get hurt in the process."

"I won't," she promised.

He eyed her as if he didn't believe her. "I'm just saying you should be careful. And if my ground beef starts disappearing again…"

She laughed at her father's mildly worded threat. "It won't. Ethan doesn't seem to be the type who'd be impressed if I plunked down a handful of raw meat in front of him." She eyed her father with love. "I never could hide anything from you, could I?"

"Not a chance, girl. You still can't." He gazed at her fondly. "Your mom would be so proud if she could see you now."

"Thanks, Dad. We both turned out well, didn't we?"

"That we did. So, what's your plan for Ethan?"

"I don't have one yet," she confessed. "But it wouldn't hurt if you slipped a comment here and there that he was the one who took such great care of Tommy."

"Will do."

"In the meantime—" she slipped off the barstool and grabbed her coffee mug "—send my dinner over to his table. He looks like he needs company."

"May I join you?"

Ethan glanced up from his dinner—the dinner that had been delivered less than thirty seconds ago. "Do I have a choice?" he asked without rancor, as Ivy set her mug and an extra place setting on the table before she slid into his booth.

"No," she said smartly, unwrapping her silverware as the

waitress who followed set a plate of the same Tuesday Night Roast Beef Special in front of her. "Thanks, Janine."

The young woman, wearing the diner's trademark uniform of a white butcher's apron over jeans and a black T-shirt, smiled. "You're welcome, Ivy. More coffee?" She held up the pot in her hand. "It's decaf."

"Please."

Ethan waited until she'd filled both mugs before he spoke. "I thought you were going straight home to bed after you left the hospital? Being so exhausted and all."

She smiled. "I got my second wind, which I can tell you from experience will only last as long as it takes to eat." She forked a bite of roast beef into her mouth, closed her eyes and groaned. "I've been waiting all day for this."

The roast beef was tender, the mashed potatoes whipped to a white froth, the brown gravy creamy and lump-free, and the green beans seasoned to perfection with bacon and onions. It wasn't a meal approved for a cardiac diet, but if one wanted comfort food it fit the menu perfectly.

Ivy, however, had turned the simple act of eating into a sensual experience, although he doubted if she knew it. For an instant he wondered if she'd make the same satisfied noises when she was making love….

He forced the mental picture of the two of them out of his head and took a deep breath to calm his suddenly awakened hormones. "It's very good," he said gruffly.

"I hope you don't mind my barging in on you, but you looked rather lonely. And since it's unhealthy to eat alone—"

Not willing to admit that he *was* ready for more than his own company, he insisted, "I'm not lonely. I'm dining alone. There's a difference."

"Not from where I was sitting."

After watching the baby and his parents, and struggling

with the painful reminder of what he'd lost, he'd been afraid Ivy had seen more than he'd wanted her to see during that particular unguarded moment when their gazes met. Clearly she had.

"You have an overactive imagination," he countered, determined to keep his demons private. "As for your 'unhealthy' comment, what medical journal published *that* scientific theory?"

She grinned. "*The Journal According to Ivy.* So, what do you think of my dad's culinary establishment? It's the best place to eat in town."

"It's the *only* place to eat in town," he pointed out as he cut his beef with a fork.

She grinned. "That makes it the best, doesn't it?" She glanced around the room. "Dad hasn't changed the decor much over the years. As you can see, he's a minimalist."

Other than an occasional framed print, the cream-colored walls were bare. White mini-blinds covered the windows, and red plaid valances provided the only other spot of color.

"But," she continued, "it made it easy when we started holding Italian Night. It would have been tough to transform the place otherwise. Adding checkered red tablecloths and rosebud vases gave us a quick but appropriate atmosphere for spaghetti and lasagna."

"When is Italian Night?"

"The first Friday of every month. I was fourteen when I had the idea, and it's done so well that Dad's continued the tradition all these years," she finished proudly. "Be sure and come in for it. But I'll warn you, there's usually a crowd. SRO—standing room only."

"I'll keep it in mind." Then, because he was curious, he asked, "You must have spent a lot of time here?"

"I was here more than at home," she admitted. "This was my

parents' livelihood, so even as a baby I had a little corner all my own. After my mom died, when I was eight, I started doing odd jobs around the place after school and on weekends. Eventually I learned everything." She leaned closer. "I even learned how to cook in that very kitchen. I'm a whiz at boiling water."

Ethan laughed, mainly because after seeing her proud expression he couldn't help himself. "Boil water? That's your claim to cooking fame?"

"I can also toss a salad with the best of them," she said, her eyes twinkling. "With skills like those, if I ever need a second career I can host my own cooking show."

"With that sort of talent," he teased, "I'm surprised you went into medicine."

"Fate had a hand in that," she said lightly. "My mother had a chronic appendix and developed peritonitis, which got me thinking about medical careers. Then, a few years later, a close friend of mine was in a car accident and was airlifted to Oklahoma City. As I watched the helicopter take off with Heather inside, I knew I wanted to be a doctor."

"Is this the Heather who's also your nurse?"

"One and the same. So when I wasn't working with Dad I hung around Walt's office, absorbed everything I could, and was drawn to working with little people instead of big ones. I promised him that if I became a doctor, I'd come back to Danton. Here I am. So, now you know my story," she said, without stopping for breath. "What about you? Why did you become a pediatrician?"

He should have known turnabout was fair play. One shouldn't pose questions if one didn't want to be on the receiving end.

"I enjoyed science, and I liked the idea of not only diagnosing problems but correcting them," he said. "My younger brother was a Type I diabetic, and my interest in medicine stemmed from that. After I entered medical school, like you, I decided I'd rather work with kids than adults." He left out references to his additional specialty, because it would generate questions that he wasn't inclined to answer.

"And your family?"

"My brother died when I was twelve, and my parents divorced after that. Eventually they both remarried, and now they each have their own families. I only see them once or twice a year. Dad lives in Phoenix, and my mother lives in Milwaukee. St. Louis was a good halfway point."

The city had been more than that. St. Louis had become his home, the place where he'd intended to develop the roots that Ivy already enjoyed. He'd met Tiffany there, gotten engaged, and with a baby on the way, life had finally been playing out according to plan.

Sadly the plan had fallen apart before it had gotten on solid footing. Now he no longer had a place he considered home, and his dreams of having a family had been blown to dust.

"But now you're in Danton?"

"I am," he agreed.

"Tell me about your vacation so far?" she coaxed. "What have you done or seen or hope to do?"

"I haven't done much of anything," he admitted. "It's been quiet. At least it was until today, when a determined lady barged up to my door."

She smiled, apparently unfazed by his description. "Quiet is overrated. Don't you know you're supposed to go home from a vacation more tired than when you left?"

"I've heard that," he said as he swallowed more of his coffee. "But I won't be going back to St. Louis."

"Oh?" She raised a sculpted eyebrow. "Where will you be going?"

Anywhere I can find finally find peace. "Haven't decided yet. I imagine I'll head south until I feel like it's time to stop."

"The children's hospital must be a wonderful employer if your vacation can last indefinitely."

A few hours ago he wouldn't have divulged any personal information, but between his satiated stomach and his lingering sense of accomplishment over Tommy Weathers, oddly enough he felt mellow enough to share the truth—or at least *part* of the truth.

He drained his coffee. "Technically, I'm not on vacation."

To his surprise she didn't seem shocked, only curious. "I wondered," she admitted. "I couldn't imagine your boss letting you disappear for three months."

"You're right; he wouldn't. Which is why I resigned. He didn't accept it, though. Instead he gave me an official leave of absence." That had been Stewart's doing, and although he appreciated his friend's gesture, Ethan knew it was a waste of paperwork. He didn't plan to go back. Not at the end of a year. Not ever.

"So you're bumming around the country for a while?"

He wasn't inclined to tell her that his "bumming around" was a permanent, not a temporary condition. "Yeah, I am. Ever since the middle of December. So I guess it's officially been about seven months."

Her gaze grew intent. "Any particular reason why you decided to take time off?"

"I wasn't fired, if that's what you're afraid of."

"I'm not," she admitted. "I'm only curious why you felt the need to exchange your stethoscope for a hobo hat."

He was beginning to regret he'd volunteered any information at all. That was what happened when he let down his guard—he said things that encouraged people to ask questions he didn't want to answer. Unfortunately he couldn't recall his words, like a manufacturer recalled a faulty product. On the other hand, if he treated the subject lightly, instead of allowing her to see how painful it was, she'd be satisfied.

"I needed a change and decided to take an extended and long overdue trip," he said simply. "I also plan to continue my life of leisure once my three weeks with you are up," he added, in case she entertained notions of turning their temporary arrangement into a more permanent one.

She smiled. "Why do I get the feeling you think I'm going to twist your arm so you'll sign on for the long haul?"

"Because I think you will," he said.

"Would it work? Twisting your arm, that is?"

"No."

"Then I won't waste my time," she said, although she sounded too innocent for Ethan to believe her. "Be warned, though, that I intend to get every ounce of work out of you that I possibly can in the meantime."

"Considering what happened tonight, I'm expecting as much."

"A regular slave-driver," she said cheerfully. "That's me."

The same waitress appeared, and refilled his mug while Ivy held a hand over hers. "No more, thanks, Janine," she said. "If I load up on decaf, I won't be able to sleep, either."

"OK." Janine addressed Ethan. "Can I get you anything else?" When he shook his head, she tore a ticket off her pad and placed it face-down on the table.

A mere moment after she'd cleared away the dishes, a familiar-looking young couple walked up. "Hello, Ivy," the woman said. "It's good to see you."

Ivy beamed at their guests, before introducing them to Ethan as the owners of the small grocery store. "Fran, Marty—you're eating late tonight, too, I see."

"We just stopped in for a piece of peanut butter pie," Marty announced. "Since we saw you, we thought we'd ask if there's anything we can do for the Ellerbes or the Weatherses."

"Barbara has the twins, so she might need a break every now and again," Ivy remarked. "If I hear of anything in particular I'll let you know."

"Do that," Fran said. She turned to Ethan. "You're the new doctor in town, aren't you?"

"For a few weeks, yes." It seemed important to establish his short-term commitment, just so no one would build any false expectations.

"We've seen you in the grocery store," Marty mentioned. "Bottled water, sandwich fixings and root beer."

"Yeah," he admitted. "I'm surprised you remember."

"We know all of our customers' preferences." Marty preened a bit. "It's how we know what to stock and what new products to try. In a place as small as ours we can't afford to fill the shelves with items that don't sell."

"Now, Marty," Fran said, "Dr. Locke isn't interested in our business habits." She turned to Ethan, her eyes shining with sincerity. "It's wonderful having you here to help Ivy. We'd hate to wear her out within the first few months she's here. In the meantime, if there's anything we can do to make you feel at home, just let us know."

"Thanks," he said.

As soon as the two moved away, he lowered his voice. "Word travels fast, doesn't it?"

"It's a small town. We don't have a newspaper, and there isn't a lot to do besides pay attention to what everyone else is doing." She smiled knowingly. "You'll get used to it."

He was accustomed to living in a city, where no one recognized him. Being the current hot topic of conversation was somewhat disconcerting. "I'm not so sure," he admitted, before he sipped his refill.

"Trust me, you will," she said. "Whatever you do, though, purchase your condoms out of town."

He nearly spewed his coffee across the table. "What?"

Her eyes sparkled as her smile spread from ear to ear. "Trust me. If you don't heed my advice, speculation will run rampant."

"I assume the same rule applies for over-the-counter pregnancy kits?"

"Absolutely."

"Thanks for the warning."

"My pleasure." She stifled a yawn. "I hate to eat and run, but my second wind just disappeared."

"I can give you a lift if you're too tired to drive."

"I'll manage, but thanks for the offer."

In spite of the dark circles under her eyes and the tired droop in her shoulders, her smile stirred something in his chest—something he hadn't felt for a long time. "I'll walk you outside," he said, suddenly wishing their time together wasn't ending.

"Afraid I'll get mugged in the parking lot?" she teased as she slid out of the booth.

He did the same, stopping long enough to toss down enough bills to cover their meals and a generous tip.

"My dinner's on the house," she said, apparently noticing the amount he'd left.

"Then the waitress just earned herself a nice tip," he said as he ushered her past a booth of giggly teenagers to the door.

"That's sweet of you, because Janine can really use the money." She waved a hand in farewell to her father, and Ethan felt obliged to do the same.

Outside, before she got into her ten-year-old car, she grabbed his hand. "Thanks again. I'll see you tomorrow, bright and early."

The sensation of her soft hand in his short-circuited his brain. "Bright and early," he echoed. But before he could tell her goodnight Janine came running out of the diner.

"Dr. Ivy," she yelled. "Dr. Ivy."

Ethan raised his hand. "She's over here,"

"Thank goodness," Janine said breathlessly. "You two have to come. One of our customers—a teenager—David Grayson—just passed out."

CHAPTER FOUR

Ivy brushed past Ethan and hurried toward the entrance, her exhaustion vanishing. "Is he choking?"

"Not that I could tell. Your dad sent me out here to find you."

"A patient of yours?" Ethan asked Ivy.

Ivy shook her head. "No. I know the family by sight, but that's all. His mom was ahead of me in high school by a few years."

Inside, Ivy found a crowd of people surrounding the boy on the floor. Her father and Millie, his other evening waitress, were crouched beside him, while his young friends hovered nearby. Two girls were wringing their hands and crying. Another watched wide-eyed and clutched the arm of her boyfriend.

Someone—her father?—had pulled tables back to allow for more room.

"Let us through," Ivy demanded, and the group parted to reveal a white-faced, drowsy fourteen-year-old, lying in a fetal position. "Everyone move back, so he can have some air."

The group collectively took three steps back.

"I'm glad you two are here," Don said, giving up his place

to Ethan. "I don't know what's wrong with him. At first I thought he'd choked on food, but he wasn't eating. Then I thought he was having a seizure, but he doesn't act like he's convulsing, either."

Ethan pulled out a chain around the boy's neck from underneath his clothing. Ivy watched as he revealed a shiny new Medic-Alert pendant.

"He's someone's patient," Ethan remarked.

She wrapped her fingers around the boy's wrist to take his radial pulse. "I'd say so, but that doesn't help us." As soon as she finished counting, she addressed his friends. "Do any of you know if he has a medical condition?"

"No," they echoed.

"Has he been ill? Or complained of being ill or feeling sick?" she asked.

Heads shook. "He mentioned he was tired and had a little bit of an upset stomach, but that's all," one of the teens mentioned. "In fact, we had to talk him into coming out with us tonight."

Ivy watched Ethan bend down over David's face, then straighten. His expression was grim.

"Call an ambulance," he ordered, as he lifted one of David's eyelids and checked his pupils.

Her father jumped up. "Right away."

"Diabetic?" Ivy guessed.

Ethan nodded. "I think so. His breath is fruity-smelling. He's probably in ketoacidosis. David? Can you hear me?"

David mumbled.

"David, are you a diabetic?"

Again, the teen mumbled.

Ivy eyed David's friends. "What was he eating?"

A long-haired brunette answered. "Same thing the rest of us were. A burger, fries, soda."

"Don't forget the pie," the other boy added. "Cherry. But he only took a few bites."

Ivy exchanged a glance with Ethan. "Glucose overload, I'd guess."

"Undoubtedly," he agreed.

"I wonder if he didn't take a large enough dose of insulin before dinner."

"Or none at all," Ethan said grimly.

While it would be nice to know, for future reference, if the boy had simply miscalculated or if he'd purposely omitted his insulin, their main concern right now was to stabilize his condition.

Immediately she looked for and found Janine. "I have a bag on my backseat. Bring it, will you?" While the waitress disappeared, she caught Ethan's questioning gaze. "I carry a glucose meter in my medical kit. It pays to be prepared."

"A regular Girl Scout."

"That's me."

Her father hurried through the maze of tables to rejoin them. "Ambulance is on its way," he huffed. "I also called David's parents. His mom said he was diagnosed as a diabetic about three months ago."

"Bingo," Ethan said, clearly satisfied to have their diagnosis confirmed. "Check his pockets. He may carry insulin."

Ivy began patting down the side pockets of David's jeans, while Ethan turned to David's friends. "Did he have a jacket?"

"Yeah." His buddy pointed to the booth. "It's over there."

"Check his pockets," Ethan repeated.

The teen scrambled into the seat and followed Ethan's instructions. "What am I looking for?"

"A vial of medicine, a syringe, glucose tablets. Anything."

The boy frantically turned the fabric inside out. "Nothing. There's nothing."

Ethan turned to Ivy. "What about you?"

She shook her head. "Same here."

Janine flew back in, breathless. "I've got it."

Ivy didn't waste time. She flung a blood pressure cuff at Ethan, knowing he would monitor the vitals while she did her part. A minute later she stabbed David's finger with a stylet, caught the large red drop of blood on a glucose strip and inserted it into her meter. Thirty seconds ticked by.

"Well?" Ethan demanded, clearly impatient.

The display lit up. "Three hundred," she said. Normal glucose was under one hundred twenty, so David had definitely exceeded the limits.

"I don't suppose you have IV supplies in your bag?" he mentioned.

Today Ivy wished that she did, although if she carried everything she might need she'd be driving a county emergency vehicle instead of her trusty old car. "Sorry. First aid stuff, mostly."

One of the girls began to wail. "He's breathing funny. Is he going to die?"

Ivy had noted David's respirations were both deep and increased. Kussmaul's respirations was the textbook term, and they were one more sign associated with diabetic ketoacidosis.

"We're doing everything we can," she told the girl. "But he needs to be in the hospital, where we can monitor him closely." The main thing was to bring down his circulating glucose level and reverse the dehydration and cellular glucose depletion before he went into an irreversible coma. A major complication was electrolyte imbalance, especially a decreased potassium level which, if severe enough, could lead to heart dysrhythmias and death.

"Ambulance is here," her father interrupted.

"OK," she ordered. "Everybody needs to get out of the way so the paramedics have room to maneuver."

The adults in the room drifted toward their tables and the teens moved about six feet away.

Two paramedics hauled in a gurney loaded down with supplies, while a local policeman stood nearby, ready to assist with crowd control.

"Ketoacidosis," Ethan told Ben Kovacs as the emergency worker crouched beside him. "His vitals are abnormal and his respirations are increased. His fingerstick glucose is three hundred. As soon as you start a normal saline IV, transport him to the E.R."

Ben nodded, and began ripping open intravenous fluid kits. "Will do."

With Ben and Ethan taking control of the situation, Ivy rose and turned to David's friends. "Why don't you all go home?" she suggested kindly. "You can check with David's parents in the morning to find out how he's doing."

"Can't we go to the hospital, too?" the calmest girl of the three asked. "You see, we feel sort of responsible, because we insisted on eating out tonight."

"I understand, but really, it will take hours before he'll be able to have visitors. I doubt if your parents will want you staying up all night."

"It isn't like we have school tomorrow," the boy beside her pointed out.

"Even so, this is a decision between you and your parents," Ivy said firmly.

"If we go home, will we be able to see him tomorrow?" the girl asked.

"Maybe for a few minutes. I'm sure he'll appreciate knowing how concerned you all were. In fact, I'll tell him the first chance I get."

Out of the corner of her eye, Ivy saw the three men move the gurney next to David's prone figure, and immediately took a position to assist. On the count of three, David was settled on the thin mattress and on his way to the waiting ambulance.

"Why don't you go home?" Ethan suggested as Ben's partner slammed the doors closed and hopped behind the wheel.

"I'm on call," she reminded him.

"That can be changed," he said. "You're dead on your feet."

Although she knew she was, especially after existing on a couple of hours of sleep every night for the last two weeks, she hated to admit her weakness—especially to her new colleague. "I'm fine." She'd no sooner said that when she stumbled on the gravel.

He grabbed her arm. "Really?" He didn't sound convinced.

"Yes, really. Anyone can trip over a rock," she said waspishly. "It doesn't mean I'm too tired to do my job. Besides, it's late. I'm sure you're tired, too."

"I've been taking life easy, remember? My three-week clock is ticking, so you might as well take advantage of it."

Ivy was tempted. Really tempted. But she hadn't given him the most basic of orientations yet! It wasn't that she didn't trust his abilities, or his intelligence to figure things out on his own, but leaving him to muddle through alone seemed so unprofessional.

"You've already done enough today," she insisted. "I can't ask you to—"

"You aren't asking. I'm volunteering. Which isn't a common occurrence. Now, what would you rather do? Argue about this or let me treat the patient?"

"We'll both go," she decided.

"Afraid I won't handle his case properly?" His tone was

mocking, but underneath she sensed his hurt. Obviously he regretted telling his story, or at least the edited and highly condensed version.

"Your skills aren't in question. I just don't understand why you're willing to get involved to the degree you have when a few hours ago you didn't care if I worked twenty-four-seven."

"Let's just say I have a special interest in kids like young David."

"Because of your brother?"

He hesitated as his gaze unflinchingly met hers. "Yes…"

His comment triggered something he'd said earlier. "Did he die under similar circumstances?" she asked, her heart going out to him.

"More or less."

She'd seen too many families split by the death of a child, and suspected that this single event had completely changed Ethan's life. "Then—"

"Let it go, Ivy," he snapped. "Now isn't the time to hash out my history. We should get to the hospital before David celebrates his next birthday."

She knew they couldn't do much for their patient over the next hour. The first step in treatment was to replace fluid and correct any electrolyte imbalances, especially abnormal potassium levels. With the IV set at a rate of one liter per hour, they still had a good portion of those sixty minutes left before they could administer insulin. The amount would be dependent upon his lab values, but they needed to be at the hospital to order the appropriate tests which would take time to perform.

"All right," she said. "Want to ride with me, or take your own vehicle?"

"I'll drive myself," he said as they passed his car and he veered off toward the driver's side.

"Then I'll see you there."

As she followed Ethan's red taillights the five blocks to the hospital, she realized that Ethan Locke might pretend to be a rough, tough and gruff man, who didn't care about anyone but himself, but underneath the obvious was a man who happened to be the exact opposite.

Ethan strode into David Grayson's trauma room, pleased to see Nancy and two of her colleagues hooking the poor boy up to the usual host of monitors and gadgets. At least he wouldn't have to introduce himself or explain his presence to these staff members. "Is it always this busy around here?" he asked, curious to hear their response.

Nancy glanced at him before she turned her attention back to David's IV. "It runs in spells. Tonight, though, we're definitely earning our salaries."

"In that case I want a stat blood glucose level, electrolytes, both serum and urine ketones, BUN and Creatinine, and arterial blood gases."

The nurse simply nodded, as if she'd expected those orders. "To save time, I already drew the venous blood samples and called out the lab tech. She should be here in a few minutes."

Ivy rushed in. "How's he doing?"

"About the same. All we can do now is wait until the lab gives us some numbers to work with."

"OK."

Ethan eyed the dark circles under her eyes and bit back a strongly worded suggestion to go home. If she wanted to stay, who was he to naysay her? After all, she was the one in charge and he was only the "hired help." In charge or not, though, she had to know her limitations, so why couldn't she just give in and let him do his job? She certainly didn't act as if she didn't trust him. She probably had some overdeveloped sense of responsibility that said she'd be deserting her patients if she stepped aside.

The problem was, if *he* had any sense he'd go home and leave David Grayson in her capable hands, as she seemed to want it that way, but she wasn't in any shape to think clearly, either for herself or her patient. She was simply functioning on auto-pilot. Interns and residents did it all the time, but they had the luxury of knowing someone else was there to catch any mistakes they might make. Right now he was her safety net, which as far as he was concerned wasn't a good thing.

She wasn't in any shape to think clearly. As that thought rattled around his brain he came to a surprising realization. For the first time in a long time he was able to focus beyond his own problems to see someone else's. It was nothing short of amazing, in fact, downright miraculous, and the reason for it was blatantly obvious.

Ivy.

Ivy had barged into his presence and had given him an hour of freedom. An hour when he'd felt…like his old self. No engulfing sadness, no sense of failure had plagued him for those sixty minutes. In fact, being with her had made him feel as if the last year hadn't existed—that he was a man with huge dreams and endless possibilities in his future.

Because of her gift—a gift she hadn't even known she'd given—he felt compelled to return the favor. But if she didn't cooperate his so-called favor only meant that both of them would be exhausted tomorrow. The main point in his favor was that he wasn't running on empty like she was, which meant he could orchestrate a few maneuvers of his own.

"Nothing we can do now but watch the clock," he said. "How about a cup of coffee?"

She rubbed her face tiredly. "Sure. Why not?"

He ushered Ivy out of the room as the brunette lab tech

rushed in, the tails of her white coat fluttering behind her as she hastened to button it over a pair of capri pants and a tank top. A male E.M.T. stood behind the nurses' station, talking on the phone, but he hung up as Ethan and Ivy approached.

Ethan stopped at the desk. "Let me know when David's parents arrive."

"They're already here," said Robert, according to his name tag. "I put them in the family room."

"OK." He turned to Ivy. "Are you up to talking to them, or—"

"Go ahead," she said. "I'm going to find some coffee."

"Fair enough."

David's parents were in their late thirties, and Ethan saw a distinct family resemblance between father and son. After introducing himself, and explaining his diagnosis, Ethan admitted, "I wish I could tell you more right now, but we're waiting for the lab results. Your son is receiving an IV now, to restore his electrolytes, and as soon as he's gotten enough fluids we'll be giving him insulin to bring his glucose down."

Mrs. Grayson shook her head. "I don't understand how this happened. He's been taking his insulin shots."

Ethan knew he had to tread carefully. "Have you seen him administer his injections lately?"

"No," she admitted. "He does it in the bathroom."

"Can he calculate the proper dosage? Does he check his blood-sugar levels regularly?"

"I'm sure he does," Mr. Grayson said. "He's been through all the instructions with Dr. Walt, his nurse practitioner and a dietician. He's fourteen, and old enough to know how important it is to take his medication and watch his diet. There has to be some other reason why he's in this ketoacidosis state you mention."

"There are a lot of possible causes," Ethan said. "Has he

been ill in the past few days, or over-exerted himself with a new sport?"

Both parents shook their heads.

"Don't worry," Ethan said kindly. "We'll straighten him out and get to the bottom of this so he can prevent it from happening again."

"Can we see him now?"

"For a few minutes," he said. "He's pretty groggy, and will probably sleep most of the night."

"When can he go home?"

"At this point I can't say," he said honestly. "It all depends on how serious his condition is and how quickly he responds to treatment."

He escorted the Graysons to their son's side, where Nancy told him that David had received the liter of fluids and she had received a verbal report of his lab results.

David's potassium level was abnormally high, as he'd expected, and his blood glucose was at two-ninety—less than when they'd tested it in the restaurant, but only by a negligible amount. His blood pH was seven point two, which was lower than normal, and meant that he was definitely acidotic.

He immediately calculated a low dose of insulin therapy in order to bring down the glucose slowly, to lower the risk of causing cerebral edema, which was a rare but serious complication in children and adolescents. Because his potassium level was high, and the insulin would cause it to fall, he didn't need to supplement David's IV with the electrolyte now—although they'd have to monitor it closely to keep it within the normal limits.

Once again he marveled at how easily he'd made the transition to treating a patient David's size. On the other hand it wasn't too surprising, because he'd vacillated between specializing in adolescent medicine and neonatology before the latter had won out. How ironic to think he'd come full circle.

"Give him a bolus of regular insulin," he told the nurse, stating the exact amount. "We'll recheck in an hour, and if his glucose hasn't dropped by fifty to seventy mg/dl, then we'll modify the dose."

"What about additional potassium?" she asked.

"The level is high right now and will fall, but we want it steady between three point three and five point five, so we'll forgo it for the moment. We'll repeat the test in two hours, and if the number falls within that range, we'll supplement then."

"Do you want to correct his pH with bicarbonate?"

"No, because his pH isn't that low, and it will correct itself as we get insulin into him."

With nothing left to do but wait for the next few hours, he went looking for Ivy and found her in the tiny staff lounge just off the E.R. She was sitting on a lumpy-looking sofa, her scuffed trainer-clad feet resting on the coffee table in front of her, sipping from a hospital mug.

"How's the coffee?" he asked as he poured himself a cup, then leaned back against the counter to drink it.

"Awful, but at this time of night what can you expect?"

He grimaced at the taste. "A European or Italian roast would be nice."

She scoffed. "Sorry, but you won't get that on a good day. I doubt if anyone would even know what you're asking for."

"Pity."

She sipped her brew again. "Did your hospital provide gourmet coffee for its staff?"

"No. Several of us in—" He stopped himself from mentioning his department. "Several of us on my floor considered ourselves coffee aficionados. Because we each took turns buying grounds when we ran out, eventually everyone developed a taste for more than the run-of-the-mill store-bought brand. One of our ward clerks worked part-time at a coffeeshop, and she often experimented when she fixed a pot." He smacked his lips, remembering. "Heavenly—that's what it was."

"Ours definitely isn't heavenly, but it packs a punch," she said, stifling a yawn. "Any lab results yet?"

He recited them for her.

"What's your treatment plan?" she asked.

"He just finished his first liter of saline, and Nancy is administering his first dose of insulin. If his glucose drops below two-fifty mg/dl by the next time we check it, we'll switch from saline to five percent dextrose."

"So now we wait?"

He nodded. "If I were you, I'd consider a nap."

Again she hesitated, but she looked less sure of her decision, especially after she yawned again. "Maybe you're right," she conceded. "An hour or two should be enough to rejuvenate a few brain cells."

Although he disagreed, he pretended otherwise. "Sounds good."

"And you'll wake me when you have the next set of numbers, right?"

Ivy needed more than sixty minutes of shut-eye; she needed about eighteen hours. But he wasn't going to tell her that. It was going to be a long night of waiting for David's condition to stabilize. It seemed pointless for both of them to stay awake.

"I will," he promised, privately vowing not to try too hard. He drained the rest of his lukewarm coffee, noting that by the time he rinsed his mug, Ivy had curled into a fetal position and was fast asleep.

Like a true medical resident, he thought with a smile. They learned to instantly fall asleep because they often didn't have the opportunity to grab more than a few winks at a time.

For several long minutes he watched her, taking in the way her eyelashes rested against her cheeks, the way her mouth had curled into the tiniest smile, the way she'd rested her face on her folded hands. She was definitely a remarkable woman, and she possessed a strong character to match. She clearly fought for what she believed, and didn't include the word *quit* in her vocabulary.

Idly, he compared her to his former fiancée and realized that even from the short time he'd known Ivy the two women were worlds apart. While it was obvious that Ivy handled more problems on a daily basis than Tiffany did in a year, and faced each and every one head-on, Tiffany did not. The premature birth of their son and his resultant medical issues had been more than she could deal with. She'd looked to Ethan to make everything "normal", and when he'd failed she'd blamed him.

Chances were, though, any other woman have responded in the same manner and held him responsible. After all, he was supposedly an expert at caring for neonates, and he took his failure personally. All the more reason to avoid a relationship, because he believed in total honesty. He refused to share his past and risk watching the light of trust die in someone's eyes again.

Frankly, he couldn't stand to see the light die in *Ivy's* eyes. Like a prisoner waiting for his release, Ethan needed to focus on the end of his three weeks, and then he could go back to his quiet, solitary existence.

He tiptoed across the room and carefully closed the door behind him as Nancy approached. "I meant to ask you earlier, do you want me to call you or Dr. Ivy in a couple of hours?"

He guided her away from the lounge's door, although he didn't think a bomb could wake Ivy now. "Do not call Ivy under any circumstances," he said. "She fell asleep on your sofa, and if at all possible I'd like her to stay that way until morning. Got that?"

She grinned. "Got it." Her smile faded. "She won't be happy if she knows what you've done."

"So sue me. I'm doing this not only for her, but for the sake of the patients."

Nancy nodded. "Do you have a phone number where I can reach you, or—"

It seemed counterproductive to drive home, especially since he lived seven miles out of town. "I thought I'd hang around here in case anything else happens—which, the way the night has gone, is entirely possible," he said dryly. "I'd rather no one bothers her unless we're completely out of our depth."

She nodded, apparently agreeable with his plan. "Feel free to use the bed in Room One. Dr. Walt considers it the most comfy of all of them, and he should know. He's spent many a night on it."

"Don't mind if I do."

"You know, if I didn't tell you before, Dr. Locke, welcome to Danton. I suspect you're just what we need around here."

Feeling long-term chains beginning to wrap around him, he tensed. "Yeah, well, I'm only here for three weeks, so don't get any ideas about making my stay longer. Walt will be back by then, and I'll be on my way."

"If you say so," she said dubiously.

"I do." Of that much he was certain. He was only helping out because of a weak moment. Nothing more and nothing less. Once he did his stint, then perhaps he'd finally find the peace that had eluded him for the past few months.

CHAPTER FIVE

IVY woke to the sound of percolating coffee and its rich scent hanging in the air. For the briefest of moments she wondered if her dad had come over early and brewed a pot for her, but as the rough weave of the white cotton blanket in her grasp registered her eyes popped open and she found herself in the staff lounge instead of her bedroom.

Now she remembered her evening… For an instant she was impressed that a few hours' sleep had so thoroughly rejuvenated her, but as soon as she saw the clock, she bolted upright.

7:00 a.m.

Where had the night gone?

Irritated because Ethan hadn't woken her as promised, she flung off her blanket and strode through the E.R. "Where's Dr. Locke?" she demanded of Nancy, who was going off-duty.

"He left about an hour ago," the nurse said.

Ivy ran her hand through her hair, knowing that she wasn't doing her tangled tresses any favors. "The Grayson boy?"

"His glucose was down to two-oh-five the last time we checked. His pH is up to seven point four, and his potassium is four point five. He's getting IV insulin, potassium chloride and potassium phosphate, and five percent dextrose in his IV fluid. Dr. Locke admitted him because David is complaining of nausea."

Everything Nancy told her fit what Ivy would have done—including keeping David for another day in the hospital. Discharging the teen before he could rehydrate on his own without an IV would only guarantee the boy would be back soon. "So where *is* Dr. Locke?"

Nancy shrugged. "Home, I guess. He said something about taking a shower before your office opened, so you'll probably see him shortly."

"He was supposed to wake me hours ago," she groused.

"He tried," the nurse said. "Honest. I watched him. You were dead to the world, though, so Dr. Locke gave up and said to let you sleep."

Ivy ran a hand over her face. *Dead to the world.* "I find it hard to believe that he couldn't wake me. I'm a very light sleeper."

"You were terribly tired," Nancy pointed out. "I thought you might wake up when he covered you with a blanket, but you slept through that, too."

Normal house noises woke her up, so she doubted if she'd slept through everything Nancy claimed she had. Unfortunately it was too late to whine and complain about the situation now. In any case Nancy wasn't responsible, but Ivy would definitely have words with the fellow who was.

"You realize, don't you," the nurse continued, "that this is the first night you've actually slept more than two hours in the last few weeks? If you ask me, you ought to be kissing his feet for taking over instead of gearing up to explode. As a matter of fact—" she grinned "—maybe you should kiss something other than his feet. I certainly would."

Ivy colored. She almost had when he'd agreed to help with the car-accident victims, but she'd learned from experience that having a relationship with a colleague was a prescription for heartache. Relationship or not, she was now indebted to him on three counts. One, for his three-week agreement; two, for treating Tommy Weathers, and three, for taking over the Grayson case so she could sleep. At this rate she'd never be able to even the score.

"If I were you," the nurse added, "I'd turn myself into something less like what my cat sometimes drags home so Dr. Ethan doesn't feel as if he wasted his magnanimous gesture."

Ivy grinned. "I look that bad?"

"Let's put it this way. If you want to impress someone, you won't."

"Then it's a good thing I don't. Want to impress someone, that is."

"Ivy, Ivy, Ivy." The forty-five-year-old nurse shook her head. "With an attitude like that you'll end up never needing more than a two-cup coffee-maker in your house. I, for one, know that a certain eligible male loves his coffee."

Ivy knew it, too. And if Ethan hung around anyone's house for long, they'd be making it in industrial-sized urns. The thought of waking up to a full-bodied brew, or the man who'd inspired it in the first place, raised her core temperature another degree.

"All right, all right. I'll go home and do what I can to make myself presentable. But I'm not doing it to impress anyone."

The nurse smiled, as if she knew Ivy was only deluding herself. Because, strangely enough, Ivy *wanted* to impress Ethan—and not with her medical skills.

"If you say so. By the way, I'm on duty tonight, and I'd be perfectly happy if you kept things quiet so I could work on my niece's baby's afghan. She's due in a month and I can only knit so fast."

Ivy chuckled. "I'll do my best."

She hurried home, which wasn't difficult because her house stood a mere block away. By the time she'd finished her shower, dressed in clean, crisp trousers and a cotton shirt, fixed her hair and slapped on the tiniest bit of make-up, she felt like a new woman. Although she intended to scold Ethan for disobeying her orders, she had to admit those hours of sleep had been life-saving. She shuddered to think what shape she'd be in today if he hadn't taken matters into his own hands.

To show her appreciation, she stopped by the grocery store on the way to work. By the time she arrived in her offices at the Danton Medical Clinic, her staff had all arrived, with their curiosities aroused.

"Sounds like you had an interesting evening after we went home." Heather's eyes twinkled. "I'm crushed you didn't call me."

"Sorry, but we barely had time to eat. It was one of those nights. Again." She explained about David Grayson.

"Yeah, well, tonight's the last night of the full moon, so maybe things will slow down around here."

"Let's hope," Ivy replied fervently. "In the meantime, we're going to make a few staff adjustments to accommodate our new physician. He doesn't want to treat babies, so keep that in mind when talking to parents. Funnel the older kids in his direction." She truly didn't believe any of the parents would balk at Ethan examining their children. After all, he'd already made a name for himself last night, and she hadn't been in town long enough to build up any real patient loyalty.

Ten minutes and two phone calls later, it was decided. A retired nurse from the hospital had agreed to help Ivy for a few weeks, while Heather would work with Ethan because she was experienced in the office procedures. Luckily the treatment rooms lined both sides of an L-shaped corridor, so he could use the cubicles on the right while Ivy commandeered the ones on the left. The arrangement might create a traffic jam at times, but it seemed like a minor inconvenience in comparison to working extra-long hours.

The receptionist and the billing clerk both disappeared into their offices as the phones began to ring. Heather, however, didn't leave.

"I want the full story, not the condensed version," the nurse warned. "After what happened last night, why do you look so good this morning after not getting any sleep? Could there be a little romantic interest simmering between the two of you?"

Ivy's skin warmed, as she wondered if her friend had suddenly developed an ability to read minds, but just because Ivy found him attractive underneath his brusque manner, it didn't mean she planned to act on it. "Don't be ridiculous. If I look better than usual it's because I dozed off in the lounge and Dr. Locke didn't wake me when he was supposed to," she grumbled, still torn between being angry or being grateful.

Heather snickered. "You're just unhappy because he knew what you needed and did something about it on his own, without asking your permission. Gracious, girl. You ought to be thanking your lucky stars he was so thoughtful. As for scolding him, I'd rethink that plan if I were you. If he was able to help that much in one evening, we'd be foolish to do anything that might send him back to his cabin hideaway."

As convinced as Ivy was that he would honor his word, she didn't want to test it. "Give me a little credit for having common sense," she said wryly. "When a gift drops into my lap, I'm not going to complain about the wrapping paper."

Heather's eyes sparkled. "He does make a pretty fine package, wouldn't you agree?"

Ivy avoided her friend's gaze. Admitting she was wildly attracted to the taciturn Ethan Locke would only plant ideas in Heather's head. After being her friend for years, Heather didn't need any help in that regard. "I haven't noticed."

"Come now," Heather scoffed. "He—"

"He'll be here any minute," Ivy interrupted. "So make a pot of this, will you?" She thrust her small bag at Heather.

The nurse peered inside. "French vanilla?" She studied Ivy with curiosity. "Trying to impress the big city doctor?"

"I doubt if he'll be bowled over by something as common as French vanilla," Ivy said dryly. "But he likes gourmet coffees, and this was the only one in the grocery store. I thought it would be a nice 'welcome to the office' gesture."

"Good plan. Too bad you didn't bring doughnuts, too."

"Let's not go overboard," Ivy said. "I haven't been around him much, but he's a loner, and if we make too big a fuss or thrust him into the limelight without warning he won't be a happy little doctor. And right now I'll give him whatever he wants for the next three weeks."

"Ah, I get it. We'll let him warm up to us first, and *then* we'll show him what small-town hospitality is."

Ivy grinned at how close Heather's statement mirrored her own plans. "Exactly. So hop to it or you'll spoil our surprise."

By the time Ethan arrived, the scent of Ivy's coffee had permeated the office.

"Good morning." His eyes reflected wariness.

"Good morning," she replied cheerfully, noting how his dark hair still looked damp from his morning shower. He was dressed casually, in a pair of black cotton trousers and a short-sleeved lime-green shirt that lay open at his neck. Freshly shaven, he smelled like a clean, but masculinely scented bar of soap. "Are you ready to get started?"

"It's why I'm here," he said shortly.

She ignored his testy comment, certain he was trying to establish boundaries, but he was too late. She'd already seen past his ferocious bark to the cautious friendliness and heart-felt compassion underneath.

"You sound like you need a morning cup of coffee," she said instead, as she led him toward the coffeepot in the tiny room they'd set up as their kitchen. "I'm sure our brew isn't up to your standards, but I bought some French vanilla grounds for you at the market this morning."

He looked stunned, as if he couldn't imagine why she would have gone to such trouble. "You did? For me?"

"Sure. Why not? It won't hurt any of us to broaden our horizons a bit. Marty and Fran also said to tell you that if you want a special blend or brand, they'll order it for you."

"Really? But I'll be leaving soon."

"Not until the end of the summer, right?"

"Possibly," he prevaricated.

"Doesn't matter." She grabbed a mug from the row of hooks above the microwave and filled it. "You're here for the next couple of weeks and that's what counts. Fran's thinking about passing out samples to their customers, and then everyone in town will develop a taste for gourmet coffees, too. So be sure and let her know a few of your favorites. Sugar or creamer?"

"Black."

"Now that we have the important stuff out of the way—" she filled a mug of her own "—tell me about David Grayson."

His blue eyes once again turned wary. "He's doing better. I called the hospital a few minutes ago and his last glucose level had dropped to one-eighty. His potassium is staying around four and his pH came up nicely."

"Did you find out why he went into DKA in the first place?" It was nice talking to a colleague who'd understand the alphabet soup jargon, which in this case stood for diabetic ketoacidosis.

"Like you, my initial thought was an infection of some sort, but I couldn't find any visible signs," he admitted. "His urine was clear, his chest sounded fine, and the X-rays didn't show pneumonia. The strep screen was negative, although it will be a few days before the culture is completed. His parents also denied that he'd had a cold, stomach flu or anything viral."

"Do you think it's a compliance issue?" she asked.

"That's my guess. I intend to have a heart-to-heart with young David tonight, and once we sort him out I think he may be able to go home tomorrow, with a follow-up visit in a couple of days."

"It sounds as if you have everything under control."

"I hope so." He paused. "Is this when you chew me out for not waking you?"

She grinned at the way he stiffened, as if bracing himself for harsh words. "I thought about it," she said lightly, "but then I changed my mind. Complaining about getting a relatively decent night's sleep doesn't make sense. Although I'm curious… Did you really try to wake me?"

A grin slowly stretched across his face. "Yes, but to be honest I didn't try too hard."

"I didn't think you did."

"Things were running like a Swiss watch. But trust me. If something had come up that I couldn't handle I would have done whatever was necessary to get you on your feet."

Somehow he seemed too confident to ever be in such a situation, but he didn't seem the type whose ego was too large to admit he'd wandered into unfamiliar territory. Her instincts whispered that she'd gotten lucky when Ethan Locke had rolled into town.

"Well, thanks again," she said. "Tonight I'm returning the favor."

"Good—because Walt might think the bed in Room One is comfortable, but I don't." He rubbed the back of his neck.

She laughed. "Walt's opinion of what's comfy doesn't match mine, either. I personally prefer a bed in a regular patient room, so keep that in mind if you ever need a mattress for a few hours."

"I will."

Voices and a sudden wail punctuated the air. "Sounds like the hordes are descending," she said. "Heather's going to act as your nurse, so if you have any questions or can't find anything, she's the one to ask."

"What about you?"

Ivy waved her hand. "I'll be fine on my own today. Heather will help me when she can, in between your patients, and starting tomorrow we'll have a temp nurse who'll assist me. Meanwhile, we've created a system where you'll use the rooms on the right. I presume you've already checked in with Ted this morning?"

"Took care of that first thing, just like I was told," he finished with a smile. "I can follow direction on occasion."

"I'm glad to hear it. Anyway, the office help will keep the coffee flowing, and my dad usually delivers lunch around eleven forty-five. Depending on how the morning goes, you may or may not have a chance to eat it, so I hope you ate your cornflakes before you came."

"And if I didn't?"

"We stash a few snacks in here. Peanuts, juice, apples and bananas. If you want something else, let Heather know. She's our snack queen. A note of warning—if you don't want to share, be sure to label it as yours."

"Just like med-school days."

"Yeah, we sleep and eat when we can."

Heather appeared at the door. "If you two are ready, I already have four rooms full of kids needing your attention."

Ivy held out her hand and Ethan took it. Amazingly enough, the same spark that had skittered down her spine yesterday, when she'd touched him, slid down her vertebrae again today. "Good luck, Doctor," she said with a smile.

"Thanks." He turned away, then stopped. "Um, Ivy? We already have a problem."

"A problem? So soon?"

He shrugged his shoulders. "My stethoscope is in a storage locker in St. Louis."

As problems went, it was one easily solved. "Is that all? Heather has a few extras in the med room. Pick one out and it's yours."

"Thanks."

But as he meandered down the hallway Ivy wondered about a doctor who'd relegate such an invaluable and personal piece of equipment—a second pair of ears, as it were—to a box containing other unnecessary items. Granted, he was on sabbatical, for lack of a better word, and probably hadn't planned to need his stethoscope while he meandered around the country, but even so, she couldn't imagine a physician treating his most important tool like an unused can opener.

When she considered how he'd wanted to be left alone, and hadn't wanted to help her when she'd first approached him, how he'd put limits on his services, she wondered if Ethan's demons were driving him completely away from medicine.

Well, she decided, squaring her shoulders, she'd seen him at work, and she wasn't going to let him turn his back on his career so easily.

Ethan dropped his borrowed stethoscope on the counter in the last exam room with some relief. He hadn't run at a frantic pace, but the steady stream of patients had ensured he was busy enough to drink his coffee on the run.

Knowing he still had to pay a visit to young David Grayson, he headed down the hall in search of Ivy, to let her know that he was leaving. He found her and her entire staff celebrating in the kitchen, with a tub of chocolate swirl ice cream.

"Did someone win the Lottery?" he asked.

Ivy laughed. The lighthearted sound struck a carefree chord that had long been buried deep inside of him and made him think of spring and children and wagging puppy dogs. "This is better."

"Better than winning a huge prize?" he asked, as Heather handed him a heaping bowl of ice cream.

All four heads nodded. "Look at the time," Ivy crowed.

He did. "It's four-fifteen. So?"

"So?" She sounded horrified. "Do you know how long it's been since we finished before seven or eight o'clock? This is practically a miracle, and we owe it all to you."

"I wouldn't go that far," he said, uncomfortable with their praise and obvious adulation.

"We saw the same amount of patients in seven hours that normally would have taken us twelve," Ivy pronounced. "If that doesn't prove you made a difference, then I'll eat my blood-pressure cuff!"

He grinned at her vehemence as he dipped into his ice cream. "OK, maybe I did have an impact, but technically I'm not finished. I need to stop by the hospital and check on the Grayson boy before I drive home."

"If things stay quiet for the next fifteen minutes we're calling it a day, too," Ivy declared. "If you like, stop by the diner on your way out of town. I happen to know Dad has fresh apple and blueberry pies today."

Although the prospect of right-out-of-the-oven pies was too good to pass up, he'd heard the mewling cry of sick infants and the affronted roar of the healthy all day. Both reminded him of what he'd lost and what he wanted to forget. Now he craved complete and utter silence from young and old alike. In fact, sitting on the back deck and listening to the birds until dark was extremely appealing. Actually, there was one thing that would top that scenario, and that would be sitting on his deck until dark *with Ivy*.

"I'll see what time I finish," he hedged, unwilling to commit, even though he didn't have anything special in his refrigerator. If he didn't stop at the diner he would definitely need to visit Fran and Marty's grocery store, because the only thing in his cupboards was a box of Shredded Wheat.

"Do that," she said. "In fact, I'll tag along with you. I have a couple of kids to see myself."

He quickly polished off his ice cream, then accompanied Ivy down the corridor connecting the clinic to the hospital. "Any more cases of whooping cough?" he asked.

"No, so let's cross our fingers that the worst is over. Strep seems to be the disease of the day."

"And swimmer's ear," he said, referring to the *pseudomonas* ear infections, now that kids spent most of their hot days in a pool.

"If it isn't one thing it's another," she agreed. "What's your plan for David?"

"I'm having a man-to-man talk with him."

"Sounds serious. Let me know if you want me to play the good cop to your bad one."

He grinned. "Who said I was going to be the bad cop?"

"You earned the role by default, because I don't frown as well as you do." She gave him a thumbs-up. "Break a leg, partner!"

Ethan watched her saunter down the hall and disappear into a patient room. What was it about her that made him feel as if the winter of his life was about to give way to spring?

Maybe he didn't want to go home to his solitary cabin right away after all... For the first time since he came to Danton he wished he'd rented a place in town, rather than several miles away.

"Can I help you, Doctor?"

The nurse's question pulled him up short. No doubt tongues would wag if anyone saw the sappy grin on his face, so he steeled his expression into more professional lines. "David Grayson's chart," he barked.

She handed it to him and, after quickly reviewing the latest lab results and nursing notes, he strode into the teen's room.

David was sprawled in bed in typical teenage fashion, clicking the television remote control with utter boredom written on his face. Ethan intended to use David's attitude to his advantage.

"How are you doing this afternoon?" Ethan asked as he closed the door.

The youth straightened and his expression brightened. "Great. Can I go home now?"

"Maybe tomorrow," Ethan said.

"Tomorrow?" David sounded horrified. "But the nurse said my glucose level was normal."

"The numbers look great," Ethan admitted, "but we need to find out why you developed problems. Especially when the dose of insulin you were taking should have been adequate."

David avoided his gaze. "I don't know what went wrong," he mumbled.

Ethan had a strong suspicion. However, he wanted David to confess. "If you don't know what went wrong, I can't send you home. The same thing could happen again."

"But...but you're the doctor and you straightened everything out. My numbers are good. You said so yourself. I'm sure once I go home I'll be fine."

Ethan stifled a smile at the boy's sincere assurance. "Perhaps," he said. "But as your doctor I need to know why your condition spiraled out of control. Your mom said you haven't been sick."

"I haven't."

"No upset stomach or a cold or—"

"I've been fine."

"Your tests certainly don't indicate any sign of infection, but I don't have all the culture results. It could take as long as two more days until the reports come in. I wouldn't want to risk missing anything, so it's best if you stay here, where we can monitor you."

"Two more days?" David sat upright. "But…but I'll miss my baseball game."

Ethan pretended to be suitably apologetic. "I'm sorry to hear that, but I just can't risk letting you go home."

David's eyes turned red, and he blinked rapidly as he crumpled the top sheet in a two-fisted grip. "I hate this diabetes," he burst out. "I *hate* it! I can't do anything I want to do!"

Ethan pulled a chair close to the bed, turned it around, then straddled it. "What can't you do?" he asked calmly.

"I can't eat with my friends whenever I want, or eat whatever they do. I can't play sports. I can't do anything on the spur of the moment because I have to live by a schedule. I'm not *normal* like everyone else!" David's chest heaved and he swiped at his nose. "It's not fair!"

"No, it's not," Ethan said. "You're one of the few kids who's learning that lesson early in life." As David brushed at his eyes, Ethan pretended not to notice. "But let's attack the things you mentioned one at a time. You claim you're not 'normal', like everyone else. Trust me when I say that everyone has a different idea of normal. As for being like everyone else, you never were and never will be—because you're *you*.

You're David Grayson, a star student and an outstanding guitar player."

David frowned. "How do you know that?"

"I have my sources," he said, not mentioning how he'd pumped David's parents for information. "You can also play sports. I hear you're an excellent basketball player and a tough shortstop."

He shook his head. "Not anymore."

"Why not?"

"Because I always have to stop and check my blood sugar, or give myself a shot in the middle of a game, because my age bracket usually plays during the supper hour. It's embarrassing. And I can't eat with the team afterward because I have to count carbs and all that junk. Do you know how many carbs are in a piece of pepperoni pizza? Everyone else is pigging out, and I'm stuck eating celery sticks!"

"I know it's tough, when everyone is eating slice upon slice and you're limited, but you can have pizza. You just need to adjust your dose of insulin a bit."

"That's what the diabetic counselor told me, but it's not working."

"You'll learn these things as time goes on. Don't expect to be an expert overnight. As for not being able to eat with your friends, you can. You just have to make the right choices. Sugar-free cherry pie looks like regular cherry pie. So does sugar-free ice-cream and jello."

"They don't taste the same," David grumbled. "And I don't *want* to make the right choices! I don't want to have to choose at all!"

"David," Ethan said gently, "no one does. No one asks to get diabetes, especially at your age, but fighting it won't make it disappear. The only thing you can do is control the situation so it doesn't control *you*, like it did yesterday."

David fell silent, as if weighing what Ethan had told him.

"Knowledge is power, son," Ethan said kindly. "The only way you're going to stay on top of this is to learn everything you can. The Internet has all sorts of Web sites that pertain to diabetes. Did you know there are a lot of Olympic athletes who have the same problem?"

David's eyes widened. "There are?"

"Absolutely. Again, go to the Internet and check it out."

The teen fell silent. "I've been skipping my shots," he admitted in a low voice.

"It's very adult of you to confess. I thought maybe you were."

"How?" the boy asked, clearly surprised as he met Ethan's gaze.

"My brother was diagnosed when he was about your age. He went through the same mental struggle you are. It's a tough break, but you're a tough kid. You can handle this."

Ethan almost saw the boy's spine stiffen and his shoulders straighten. "You think so?"

"Anyone who can admit their failures can do anything."

"I didn't want the guys to think I was doing drugs when they saw me with needles."

"Tell them the situation," Ethan advised. "I'll bet none of them will bat an eye. A few probably have relatives who take injections, too. And who knows? If you should ever get into trouble by accident, your friends can help you."

David slowly nodded. "OK. I'll take my stuff with me and I won't skip my shots."

"Promise?"

"Yeah."

"In that case," Ethan rose off his chair, "I'll discharge you in the morning. But—" David immediately whooped, and Ethan smiled as his ears rang from the noise. "But," he emphasized, "I'll expect to see you in my office on Monday."

"I'll be there, Dr. Ethan," David promised.

As Ethan stepped out of David's room, he ran into Ivy. "Everything OK?" she asked. "We heard the shouts, and I didn't know if he was murdering you or vice versa."

"Murder? You have a very suspicious mind, Doctor."

"Only because I don't want to lose my partner after the first day. Spare doctors don't grow on trees, you know."

"Then you're in luck. I'm still in one piece. Slightly deaf—" he rubbed one ear "—but everything else is working."

She grinned. "Perfect."

As she threaded one arm through his, he realized that certain body parts were working far better than he'd expected after a long celibate existence. He told himself as she hung on to his arm and chattered away that he'd respond the same if he felt any other woman's softness and smelled any other woman's spicy orange scent.

He was lying. Only Ivy could do this to him. Only Ivy could bring enough sunshine to chase his mental demons into the darkness, where they belonged. Only Ivy could instill hope and make him feel like a whole man instead of a wreck.

Tell her, a little voice commanded.

He should, but the risk of Ivy turning away from him as Tiffany had was too great. For now, right or wrong, he wanted to let things ride and enjoy these precious moments—because who knew how long they would last?

CHAPTER SIX

"DAD, you can't do this by yourself," Ivy protested as soon as she arrived at the diner and saw her father trying to take care of the counter, act as cashier, and wait on the tables that Janine wasn't able to cover.

Her father scoffed. "I've done it before. I can do it again."

"But, Dad. This is ridiculous. If you need more help, you should hire some."

"I don't need more help. Millie called in sick. It happens. We'll get by. Wednesday nights usually aren't that busy."

"But you shouldn't just 'get by'. You should—"

"Ivy," he warned, "we'll have a much more enjoyable dinner hour if you aren't hounding me."

"You're right. I won't hound you. I'm going to help." She strode into the kitchen, grabbed a clean apron from a hook near the door, and returned wearing it.

"For heaven's sake, girl," he sputtered. "I didn't send you to medical school so you could wait tables."

"And I didn't go to med school to watch my father die from exhaustion or a heart attack." She dug in a drawer underneath the cash register and pulled out an order pad. "I'll help as long as I can, but I'm on call."

"Been on your feet all day, and now you're going to wait

tables," her father groused. "It isn't right. It just isn't right. Your mother, God rest her soul, would—"

"Do the same thing," she said firmly. "I remember the long hours she put in, so don't argue."

He sighed. "How was your first day with a partner?"

She grinned. "Can't you tell? I'm here, and it's barely five-thirty."

"Slow day at the office?"

"Are you kidding? It was business as usual, but we were able to see twice as many kids in nearly half the time."

"That's great, Ivy. But it doesn't mean I want you moonlighting in my diner."

"I'm not moonlighting, Dad. I'm helping you out for a few hours. You'd do the same for me if you could."

"That I would," he agreed. Then, as the door opened and six people walked in, he added, "If you're going to work, you'd better get started."

In no time at all Ivy fell into the rhythm she'd developed when waiting tables as a youngster. Although Janine had expanded her section, which made Ivy's the smaller of the two, Ivy still felt as if she needed an extra pair of hands.

When Ethan slid into one of her booths nearly an hour later, she greeted him with a coffeepot. "It isn't gourmet, but it's strong and hot," she told him cheerfully.

He eyed her. "Taking up a second career so soon?"

"Not hardly. Dad's waitress called in sick, so I'm helping out for the dinner rush. What can I get you?"

"A double cheeseburger, French fries, and a piece of the pie. To go," he tacked on.

"Your fries will be cold by the time you get home."

"Won't be the first time."

Ivy scribbled his order in shorthand. "OK. It'll be about fifteen, twenty minutes."

By the time Ethan's order was ready Ivy's customers were lingering over dessert, so she carried his meal, as well as hers, to his booth. "I haven't done that in a long time," she said as she slid onto the cushioned seat.

He stared at his plate. "I thought I asked for mine to go."

"You did, but if you left I'd have to eat alone. You seem too chivalrous to want that to happen." She drizzled salad dressing over her lettuce.

Wearing a half-smile, he drew what seemed like a defeated sigh as he bit into his burger. "Do you always decide what other people should and shouldn't do?"

"Not always—which is why I'm asking what you have planned for Saturday instead of telling you."

"What's happening this weekend?"

"Danton's Annual Frontier Days Rodeo," she said importantly. "I'd like you to accompany me."

"I'm not a rodeo fan."

"You don't have to be. If you don't want to watch the bull-riding, calf-roping or other events, there are all sorts of booths to visit, filled with crafts, Western wear and gear, and plenty of good food. In the evening there's square dancing." She leaned closer. "As added incentive, period dress isn't required." As he hesitated, she pressed on. "Come on. It'll be fun. After working hard this week, you deserve to see another side of Danton."

He wore a long-suffering expression. "I don't have a choice, do I?"

"Not really. You're a pillar of the community now. You have to put in an appearance."

"A *temporary* pillar."

She waved aside his comment. "Whatever. A pillar is a pillar. So you'll pick me up about noon?"

"Noon on Saturday. OK."

"Don't forget."

"I don't think you'll let me," he said dryly.

"Great." She glanced at the nearby tables; she'd neglected her father's customers long enough. "I'll be right back." She slid out of the booth, poured more coffee and refilled soft drinks for those who wanted them, gave tickets to those who were finished, and began clearing dirty dishes.

Ethan watched her work as he polished off his meal. From the way people responded to her wide smile and sincere greetings, he didn't doubt she'd completely change the fabric of their medical establishment to implement all the services she wanted to provide. She was the sort who simply believed she could accomplish miracles and no one had the heart to say no.

She slid back into the booth as he forked the first bite of blueberry pie into his mouth. "How's the pie?"

"Delicious."

"Now you know why I don't cook," she said. "I can't compete."

"Oh, you can't tell me you didn't pick up a few tricks from your dad."

"I did, but cooking for one is about as much fun as eating alone. Wouldn't you agree?"

"Yes, but some of us cook out of self-preservation. Cold cereal and frozen dinners get old fast."

Don appeared at their table. "How was dinner?"

"Excellent," Ethan told him.

"Good." He turned to Ivy. "I hate to interrupt, but the family in the corner over there needs your help."

"What's wrong?" she asked.

"The little one—about two, I'd say—is fussy and looks feverish. And she has a horrible cough. They need a doctor, Ivy, but I can tell they're down on their luck. Said they're headed to Oklahoma City, where they have family, but I'm not sure what shape their little one will be in by the time they get there. Would you take a look? Give them a bit of free advice or a few drug samples? It may be nothing, but…"

"I can't treat their child if they don't want me to, Dad," she said gently.

"They do," he insisted. "When I mentioned my daughter was a doctor, and just across the room, I could see the hope in their eyes. But they're too proud to ask, and they can't afford a trip to the E.R. If it's more than a cold, maybe you could see them in your office?"

Don had phrased it as a question, but Ethan had the sneaking suspicion this wasn't the first time he'd suggested such an arrangement.

"All right." Without any hesitation, Ivy slid out of the booth and headed toward the couple across the room.

Ethan watched her, conscious of her father doing the same. "Does this happen often?" he asked, seeing her press the back of her hand to the child's forehead.

"A couple of times a year," he said. "I see a lot of kids come through here with their parents, and I can usually spot a sick one a mile away. Usually I tell them what a wonderful hospital we have and they go there, but once in a while we get some who don't have enough money for a meal, much less an expensive E.R. bill. I know I shouldn't make more work for my daughter, but she'd be upset with me if I didn't let her use her gift. Because that's what her knowledge and skills are," he said firmly. "A gift."

Funny thing, but Ethan hadn't considered his former and currently temporary profession in that light before. In his case, though, his so-called gift had failed where his own son was concerned. He watched Ivy spin around and take off her apron as she rejoined them.

"Sorry to bail out on you, Dad, but I have to go."

"What's wrong?" Ethan asked.

"High fever, sore throat, malaise."

The symptoms added up to a diagnosis. "Strep?"

"Probably. The sooner I give her an antibiotic, the better."
She turned toward her father. "Oh, and Dad? Call the motel
and reserve a room for the Schultz family. They don't know
it yet, but they're spending the night, so I can check on their
daughter in the morning before they continue their trip."

"I'll take care of it right away." Her father headed toward
the wall phone behind the cash register at the counter.

Ethan grabbed her arm, halting her in her tracks. "Ivy?"
he began, before words failed him. He wanted to tell her not
to care too much and drive herself into the ground, but he
sensed she wouldn't pay attention. She had a heart big enough
to want to save the world without counting the cost to herself.
From personal experience, he didn't want her so emotionally
tied to her patients that when the unthinkable happened she
wouldn't be able to cope.

"Yes?" she asked impatiently.

He opened his mouth to tell her all those things, but he
couldn't. He hadn't known her very long, but he'd seen
enough of her nature to know that asking her not to care
would be like asking the sun not to rise or the wind not to
blow. Her concern for others was knit into her bones; she
didn't have a choice.

"Nothing," he said instead. "You'd better go. They're waiting for you."

This time she paused. "I know what you'd like to say,
Ethan, because I can see it in your eyes. You want to tell me
to let someone else handle them. But there *is* no one else."

"Ivy, I—" he began.

She continued as if he hadn't spoken. "Oh, I could call

Walt's physician assistant, because she sometimes takes calls for me, but she's as swamped and as tired as I am."

"I—"

Her voice grew more insistent, almost accusatory as she continued. "You had the luxury of handing your patients to someone else, knowing they would be cared for while you're gallivanting around the country, but I don't. I *have* to do this. If you don't like it, too bad, because I'm going to—"

He stopped her the only way he knew how.

He kissed her.

What began as a quick, hard meeting of lips soon whetted his appetite for a longer, more lingering variety. As he held a steady grip on her forearms and inhaled her orange-blossom fragrance, the notion of running his fingers down her spine and pressing her against him threatened to overpower him. But a small remnant of his sanity reminded him of their audience.

He reluctantly stepped back, realizing that, contrary to his earlier belief, one kiss was not enough. Instead of satisfying his curiosity, the kiss that had lasted only a few seconds had made him want more.

As he watched her stand motionless, knowing he'd momentarily rendered her incapable of speech or action inflated his masculine ego. "Your patient is waiting," he reminded her gently.

The glazed-over look in her eyes disappeared, suggesting she'd mentally regrouped. "I have to go," she said, sounding apologetic.

"I know. Try not to save the entire world tonight, though," he advised lightly. "Leave a few patients for me to see tomorrow."

She nodded, as if her thoughts were still scattered, then turned on one heel and approached the family waiting near the restaurant door.

"Follow me to my office," she told them crisply, as if nothing untoward had happened, "and we'll see what's wrong with your daughter."

Alone, Ethan suddenly felt at loose ends, but there wasn't any point in staying. He dug in his back pocket for his wallet and pulled out a credit card as he, too, headed for the cash register.

"You don't look too happy," the older man remarked as he swiped Ethan's card.

His temper simmered. "I'm not. If Ivy keeps this up she'll wear herself out, and then who's she going to help? No one, that's who!"

"We do what we can," Don said simply. "If you think the kid business is booming, just imagine what it's like to take care of our three thousand plus adults. Danton may be small, but it could always use a few more professionals such as yourself." His tone sounded hopeful.

"I'm not planning to stay." Ethan repeated his most often used sentence.

"Plans can change. Few things are etched in stone, if you catch my meaning."

"I do. But once Walt returns, my job here is done."

Don handed him a pen and the receipt to sign. "You seem fond of my daughter."

If Don Harris knew that Ethan's feelings toward Ivy didn't come close to fondness but lay in a more hot and heavy direction, he'd probably throttle him.

"I am." Ethan unflinchingly met the older man's gaze, aware of how Ivy's father and everyone else in the diner had probably seen him kiss her.

Mr. Harris nodded, as if Ethan had confirmed what he already knew. "As a kid she collected strays. Didn't matter what it was—dogs, cats, rabbits, birds, even a turtle or two.

She found them all homes, but every time she sent them away—whether it was to a friend's house or back to the wild—it took a long time for her to get over it."

"Your point is?" Ethan asked.

"If you're not planning on sticking around, then don't start what you can't or won't see to the finish. She deserves a fellow who's going to cherish and support her every day of the week, because she's not going to keep strict office hours."

"From what I've seen so far, I don't think she knows what office hours are," Ethan said wryly.

"Kids don't get sick according to a schedule," Don agreed. "Of course, if she hooks up with another doctor who can balance things out, then we'd have a whole different story...."

Ethan hid his smile. First he'd been warned off; now he was being encouraged. The truth of the matter was that everything hinged on him staying in Danton, and he couldn't make that commitment when he didn't know if he wanted to practice medicine at all.

Yet the thought of coming home to Ivy, or being there when *she* came home, was both tempting and scary. He'd had that dream in his grasp and it had slipped away. He wouldn't survive if he lost someone he loved again.

Much as Ethan would like to be the one she leaned on, he wasn't the man for the job.

Ethan slipped his credit card back into his wallet. "Thanks again for dinner. It was great."

Don hefted a plastic tub in his arms and headed for the nearest table still covered with empty dishes. "Come back anytime."

Remembering Ivy's concern for her parent, Ethan stopped him. "Should you be doing that?"

Don laughed. "Don't tell me Ivy's got you worrying about me, too? The day I can't bus tables is the day I'll be pushing up daisies."

"Can't those wait?"

Don stacked the plates and saucers with a clatter. "For who? And for when? Dishes have to be done before we can open tomorrow, because one thing I won't do is serve on paper plates. And if I know Ivy," he went on to say, "she'll hurry back here to help close the place instead of going home and crawling into bed. The more I do before she walks through those doors, the sooner she'll go where she belongs."

Ethan instantly made a decision, and then nudged Don aside. "I'll fill in for her while you do something else. Maybe by the time she shows up we'll both be done, and we can *all* go home and get a decent night's sleep."

Don blinked his surprise. "You're willing to help?"

"I offered, didn't I?" Ethan began filling the tub with silverware and tumblers. "Just don't ask me to wait on people. I've never done that before."

"You've eaten in a restaurant, haven't you? Just write down what people ask for and be as detailed as you like. Create your own shorthand, if that helps. Nothing to it." Don stripped off his apron and handed it to Ethan. "You'll need this so you don't dirty your fancy duds. As soon as you bring me a load, I'll start the dishwasher."

"Fair enough." But by the time Ethan moved to the next table Don still hadn't moved.

"Aren't I doing this right?" he asked, wondering if there was a special trick to clearing off tables.

"Oh, no. You're doing great." Don wrinkled his face as he scratched his head. "I'm just a bit puzzled. If you're trying to earn some brownie points—"

"I'm not." Ethan stacked more plates inside the tub. "Helping you will take a load off Ivy so she can get a good night's sleep, and in turn she'll be able to do her job tomorrow, leaving less work for me."

"Then you're doing this for yourself?"

Ethan thought a moment. "Yeah. I am."

"Just like you let her sleep the other night while you dealt with the Grayson boy?"

Ethan grinned. "Yeah."

Don laughed so loud the few remaining customers looked in their direction. "If you want to believe your motives are purely selfish, you go right ahead, son. If you ask me, though, you have the same problem I do."

Ethan grew wary. "Which is?"

"We both need to watch over Ivy as best we can," he said simply, before his smile faded. "I can feed her, but I can't help carry her patient load. If you leave, what then?"

It was the million-dollar question for which Ethan didn't have an answer. It also paired well with Don's admonition not to start something he wouldn't finish.

Those things ran through his mind as he tossed and turned half the night, until he gave up and stood on the deck behind the cabin in his boxer shorts. Moonlight illuminated the grassy yard and shadows clung to the tree line surrounding the house. Crickets chirped, an owl hooted, and every now and again he heard a rustle in the bushes.

What would this place be like when the temperature dropped and snow covered every inch? More importantly, would he be here to see the leaves turn or the snow fall? If he got back on the road and kept heading south he'd winter in Texas, but was that what he wanted? At the moment he couldn't think that far ahead. Hell, he didn't even know what he would do after the next three weeks.

One thing was certain. Ivy had given him some breathing space. She'd accepted his conditions and taken what he could give her without asking questions that he wasn't willing to answer. Yet sometimes he caught her studying him, as if she'd somehow sensed his hurt and was simply waiting for him to find the courage to trust her with his secrets.

With any luck at all she'd never learn them. He couldn't bear to see the condemnation in her eyes once she discovered the depth of his failure.

At one-thirty he yawned, and knew if he didn't go to bed, Ivy would be covering for him in the morning instead of the other way around. He had time for a relatively decent night's sleep as long as he didn't replay their kiss, or remember her scent or her soft skin during that unbelievably short second when he'd indulged his fantasy and felt like a whole man again....

By the time Ivy dragged herself into the office the next morning, she still felt somewhat uncertain about what she'd do or say when she saw Ethan for the first time since they'd parted last night. After jumping to conclusions and reading the riot act to him, then being kissed, and then learning over her breakfast cinnamon roll that he'd stayed to help her father at the diner, she didn't know if she should apologize, thank him, or run and hide in embarrassment. A combination of all three was probably in order, but if the truth were known, she wouldn't mind if he kissed her again.

On the other hand, if a simple and brief encounter was able to scramble her brains so effectively, she could hardly imagine what it would be like if he kissed her as if he meant it—or what she'd experience if they let it progress to a natural conclusion.

As crazy as it sounded, and as impossible as it seemed, Ethan Locke filled an empty spot inside of her—the spot that friends and family simply couldn't satisfy. The man she'd dated when she had been able to spare the time as a pediatric resident had come close, but even with him something had been missing. Which was why, when he'd decided to join a metropolitan pediatrics practice, she'd been able to send him off with her blessing and only a few regrets.

In the space of a few days she already knew that she wouldn't be able to do the same with Ethan. The defining moment had come immediately after her father had mentioned Ethan's volunteer work at the diner. He could have gone on home and spent the rest of his evening relaxing, but he'd shelved his ego to do something humbling for a man he hardly knew. If she hadn't been attracted to him before now, his actions would have ensured it. In fact, she could honestly say she was falling in love.

She was falling in love with a man who was running from his past and from himself. A man who would be gone in a few weeks. Oh, he might stick around Danton until the summer ended, but he would eventually leave to continue his "extended vacation."

Would he ever find the place he sought? A place that brought him peace and made him want to stop drifting like a wind-blown seed?

For a woman whose roots ran deep, she'd be foolish to emotionally tie herself to a man who had none. She couldn't fall in love with him without tearing herself up in the process. If she couldn't fix whatever had caused him to give up everything he'd once held dear, he'd walk out of her life as quickly as he'd walked into it.

"Good morning." Ethan joined her at the coffeepot.

"Good morning," she said, sipping the brew in her mug to give herself time to redirect her wayward thoughts.

"Long night?" he asked.

She felt his gaze search her face and stifled a sigh. He wouldn't see her at her best this morning—which was a shame, considering his gesture last night. "Yes and no. After

I sent the Schultz family to the motel—Annika's strep test instantly turned positive, by the way—I got called to the E.R. for an asthma attack. After that every couple of hours someone from the hospital called with a question. For some strange reason I had trouble falling back to sleep." She grinned. "To top things off, I even got a wrong number."

He shook his head. "You're too nice. The staff should be trained not to call you except in extreme emergency."

"Most of them are," she admitted. "But normally a phone call doesn't keep me awake. Last night was an exception."

"Any particular reason why?"

She could have listed any number of excuses, but honesty—at least to a point—was the best policy. "I had a hard time deciding if I should apologize for ranting at you or—"

"Or slap me for kissing you?" he prompted, raising an eyebrow.

She smiled softly, wishing she was forward enough to tell him she'd love a repeat experience. "Never that. Anyway, I'd like to apologize—"

"Accepted."

"And thank you for helping Dad at the diner last night."

He looked surprised. "News travels fast."

"Dad told me this morning when I stopped by. I think he's still stunned by what you did. In fact, be prepared if he tries to hire you away from me," she finished lightly.

He chuckled. "Adding 'busboy *extraordinaire*' to my curriculum vitae will be just the thing it needs to impress prospective employers."

"One never knows what skills will come in handy," she said lightly, before she yawned. "Excuse me. I can't get moving this morning."

"When's the last time you had a day off?"

"I can't remember that long ago." She grinned. "I think it was sometime before I moved back to Danton. Six, eight weeks?"

"Then you're overdue." He took the mug from her hand. "I've already checked our appointment calendar. Heather tells me it's a relatively slow day, so go home and take a nap. I'll see you around noon," he finished gruffly.

The notion of playing hooky held more temptation than a double chocolate fudge ice cream sundae, but it was impossible. "It's sweet of you to offer, but I'll take my day off on Saturday. We have a rodeo date, remember?"

"Yeah, we do."

"Besides, I can't leave now. The Schultzes are coming in before they head out of town. Then I have several well-baby check-ups scattered throughout the morning."

"What about this afternoon?"

"You aren't going to be happy until I go home, are you?"

"How did you guess?"

"What if I promise to try to get away early today?"

"And take an extra-long lunch hour?" he pressed.

"How long is extra long?"

"A couple of hours."

"One hour," she countered.

He let out a long suffering sigh. "If that's the best you can do."

"Actually, I can do one better," she said airily. "If I skip out early this afternoon, how about coming over to my place for dinner tonight?"

His eyes brightened, and she hoped the prospect of her company was as enticing as that of a home-cooked meal. "What time?" he asked.

"We probably won't eat until six, but you're welcome to drop in as soon as you finish here."

"It's a deal. But I thought you could only boil water and toss salad."

She grinned. "Don't worry. You won't go home hungry."

As much as she knew she was playing with fire, she couldn't squelch the one thought that popped into her head and sent a shiver of anticipation down her spine.

Maybe he wouldn't go home at all.

CHAPTER SEVEN

FROM the moment Ethan talked Ivy into leaving, he was torn between counting the hours until he would see her again and calling to cancel their dinner date. He would return to his old hermit habits in less than three weeks, so it seemed pointless for her to invest so much of herself in a man who couldn't possibly give anything back. He was a fool to accept her generous invitation when he knew nothing could or would come of it in the long run.

However, in spite of his head listing a hundred reasons why he should simply go home and steer clear of her life and her problems when he had his own to solve, his heart wouldn't allow him to reach for the phone.

He was simply lured by a home-cooked meal, he told himself. He would have gone to Heather's house if she'd invited him, too.

Deep inside of him, though, he knew otherwise. The prospect of food was merely the whitewash to cover his desire to spend the evening with Ivy. He wanted another opportunity to kiss her, but this time he wanted to do it slowly and completely, and with the proper mood, instead of conducting a sneak attack that caught her by surprise. He wanted to feel like his old self, to be distracted by a beautiful woman's smile so that he could forget everything that had gone wrong…at least for a little while.

Some might accuse him of using her to achieve his own ends, but she'd invited *him* to dinner, which meant she wasn't immune to him, either. Although, regardless of their individual motives, he couldn't show up on Ivy's doorstep empty-handed, so he detoured to the diner.

"Do you have any peanut-butter pie?" he asked Don.

"Freshly made," the older man said cheerfully. "I'll box a slice for you."

"Actually," Ethan said slowly, suddenly aware his request could raise a few questions, as well as a few eyebrows, if anyone knew his destination, "I'd like the whole pie."

"Oh. Well, that's even better. You must have developed a taste for it, like Ivy has. That girl could eat it every meal and still ask for seconds."

"Really?" Ethan already knew it was Ivy's favorite, because she'd ordered a piece every time he'd seen her here, but he didn't feel comfortable admitting he would be sharing it with her. After all, Ivy might want to keep a few secrets from her dad—especially the identity of her private dinner guests.

"Yeah. You're sure you want the whole thing? That's a lot of pie for one fellow to eat by himself."

"I'm positive." Ethan whipped out a bill to pay him.

"Good thing I made two of them today," Don mentioned. "Otherwise I'd have a few other unhappy customers."

"Good thing," Ethan echoed.

Don boxed the dessert and handed it to Ethan. "Enjoy. And enjoy the stir-fry, too."

Ethan was puzzled. "Stir-fry?"

A knowing smile grew on Don's face. "I guessed Ivy was going to show off her cooking skills when a round steak disappeared from my freezer, along with all the broccoli from my salad bar and my Chinese cookbook. You picking up her favorite pie confirms my suspicions."

"Oh."

"She hasn't been able to pull the wool over my eyes yet," he crowed. "But she's tried a time or two. And don't let her fool you about her cooking abilities. That girl knows her way around a kitchen."

Ethan laughed. "I thought it was odd for a girl who'd grown up in a restaurant to only be able to boil water and toss salad."

"Oh, my, yes, she can work wonders. So you two enjoy your dinner. But whatever you do, don't mention you talked to me. She'd be upset if she knew I spoiled her surprise."

"And you don't want to hurt her feelings?" Ethan guessed, aware that he'd fallen victim to the same protective streak.

"Exactly."

"I won't say a word," he promised.

Ethan drove to Ivy's house, feeling a bit like a co-conspirator, but what surprised him most was his willingness to assume that role. For the first time since he'd begun working with Ivy he was beginning to think it might not be as easy to cut these gossamer ties as he'd first believed.

But that was an issue to deal with days from now, he decided as he parked and strode up the walk. For the next few hours he was going to push the past into the back of his mind and enjoy the moment….

"Hi," he said, as soon as Ivy answered the door with a welcoming smile that made him feel as excited as a kid on Christmas morning. "I wanted to contribute to the meal, so I brought dessert." He handed her the box.

"You didn't need to, but thanks. I didn't have time to whip anything together, so now we won't have to go for ice cream."

Ethan followed her through the house to the kitchen and

dining area, aware of the way her yellow-striped sundress accentuated her curves, clung to her hips, swirled around her long legs, and revealed miles of skin across her shoulders and arms. He swallowed hard, and shifted his weight to ease the sudden strain in his trousers.

She bent at the waist to slip the pie into the refrigerator. "What do you think of my place?"

His attention remained riveted on his hostess's graceful movements and lithe form. "It's nice," he said inanely.

"Nice?" She straightened, then faced him. "It's sweet of you to say so, but either you have absolutely no fashion sense or you're one of those guys who doesn't notice his surroundings."

She was wrong on both counts. While he couldn't claim to be an interior decorator, he watched enough home-improvement television shows these days to know what was pleasing to the eye. At this particular moment, though, the room had faded into black-and-white insignificance, while the woman in front of him stood out in vibrant, living color.

"So be honest," she continued. "The furnishings and appliances are outdated, and the decor is awful, but I'll change all that when I have the money, time and energy."

He tore his gaze from what he considered the one bright spot and took a minute to glance around the seventies-style kitchen, with its old-fashioned cabinets, worn countertop, and flooring that should have been replaced a decade ago. "You have a lot of work ahead."

"What an understatement. But I fell in love with the floor plan. The house as a whole is sound, which made it easier for me to decide to tackle the cosmetic issues myself. I redecorated the bedroom before I moved in, though, because the orange wallpaper and shag carpeting was more than I could handle," she admitted. "Dad and I painted it a cool mint-green, and we replaced the carpeting with a fake hardwood floor and an area rug. I'll take on the living room when Walt gets back and I have more time."

He had the sneaking suspicion she wouldn't gain the extra hours she thought she would. While some of Walt's patients would return to his practice, Ethan imagined most of the parents would prefer to have a younger, more up-to-date specialist overseeing their children's care instead of an elderly GP.

"Have you heard from him?" he asked.

"No, but I don't expect to. He checks in with Jed now and then, and Jed keeps me posted."

"What if he doesn't come back?" he asked tentatively.

"Danton is his home," she said simply. "He'll be back. Although, between you and me, I wouldn't be surprised if he decides to slow down and only work a few days a week. If that happens, I'll be in trouble," she finished ruefully. "Unless, of course, I can interest you in sticking around for the next twenty or thirty years?"

She looked positively hopeful, and he hated to dash those hopes but he didn't have a choice. He might be currently functioning all right on his limited medical practice, but he wasn't ready to put himself to the test and risk failure. He was a man without a future, and because of it he had to go just as she had to stay. "Sorry. Three weeks is my limit."

"If you change your mind, my offer is still open," she said. "But enough shop talk. Are you ready for dinner?"

Aware of how his stomach was gnawing at his backbone, he smiled. "I thought you'd never ask."

"In that case, would you like to sit out here, and take in the view of my weeds, or enjoy the ambience of my ancient and color-challenged kitchen?"

Ivy's presence provided all the ambience he needed. "I'll

help you," he said, rising to follow her inside. "I'm relatively handy with a knife."

"That's nice to know, but I diced and sliced my ingredients earlier this afternoon."

He eyed her as she retrieved bowls of vegetables from the refrigerator. "Instead of napping, I suppose?"

"Actually, no. I came home at three, when you all but shoved me out of the door." She grinned as if to soften her complaint. "I slept for about an hour and half, and then got started. Thank goodness you thought of dessert because I didn't have time. I can't wait to have a slice."

"Maybe we should eat it first. Life is short, you know."

"Vegetables before sweets in my house," she said. "That's the rule my dad enforced, and the one my kids will live by, too."

A mental picture of a little girl wearing her mother's magical smile appeared. "Already planning a few offspring, are you?" he asked.

"Someday," she said. "When the right man comes along. Pass the peanut oil, please?"

As she began to heat her wok, Ethan warned himself not to ask. But curiosity drove him. "And what's your idea of the right man?"

She dumped the sliced beef into the hot oil with a sizzle. "I don't know. I haven't really given him specific traits."

"Give it a try. Professional or blue-collar?"

She paused, her wooden spoon poised in mid-air. "It doesn't matter, as long as he enjoys what he's doing and understands the demands of my own career. I imagine him as being solid, dependable, selfless—someone I can lean on when I need to. He'll have to like living in Danton, and he has to fit into the community. Other than that, I really don't have any other expectations."

"None whatsoever?" he asked.

"He also has to curl my toes from time to time," she said with a smile. "As well as have the patience of a saint, because I'm the teensiest bit strong-willed."

Thinking of how she'd taken the initiative to ask a perfect stranger for help, he had to agree. But, strong-willed or not, whoever her future Mr. Right was, he would have to be a regular paragon. "You aren't asking for much, are you?" he asked facetiously.

"Hey, it's my dream fellow. I can make him as perfect as I want. What about you? What sort of woman are you looking for?"

He thought about Tiffany. "I'm not looking for anyone."

"Oh, come now. Men are *always* looking. You must have a few specifications in mind."

He shrugged, although his thoughts immediately turned in that direction. He had a few essential characteristics, but none he could share without divulging his past. The ability to forgive headed his list, but if he couldn't forgive himself he couldn't expect the woman in his life to do the same.

"Not really," he said, watching her stir the meat before adding the vegetables. "One can't settle down with a wife when drifting from place to place."

"I suppose not. Do you think you ever will? Settle in one place?"

"I like to think I will," he said, once again noncommittal. "Someday. When it's time." Then, to stave off any difficult questions she might pose, because he sensed they hung on the tip of her tongue, he asked, "Why did you decide to set up your practice here?"

"People needed me," she said simply. "I already knew Dr. Walt had more than he could handle. And everyone in town was always so supportive when I talked about becoming a doctor that I never considered going anyplace else."

"You're fortunate," he said. "In fact, I envy you having a place to come home to and knowing where you belong."

"Home is where you make it," she said softly.

How well he knew that. He'd tried to establish one in St. Louis, but had failed. "I'm one of those people who're inherently unable to develop long-lasting roots," he said lightly.

"I don't believe that." Her voice was firm. "As a person who knows how difficult it is to encourage plants to grow, I think you just haven't achieved the right mix of raw ingredients."

"I suppose you're going to tell me that I just need a soul mate beside me?"

She shrugged. "It couldn't hurt, could it? If you add living in a community as perfect as Danton," she grinned, "who knows what you could do?"

Who knew, indeed? For an instant he was tempted to spill his story and explain she was wrong, but he couldn't. It had been so long since someone had trusted him, and he didn't want to watch that faith fade once Ivy knew the truth. It was easy to suggest the fault for not having a place to call home rested on the whims of fate—not meeting the right woman, or being in the wrong place at the wrong time—but he couldn't place the blame on any of those scenarios.

His problem lay within himself, and it always would until he escaped his past.

Ivy had a hunch that Ethan had been close to divulging a few of his secrets, but just as she'd thought she was about to punch through his defenses another layer had slammed into place.

For the rest of the evening their discussion centered on topics that were personal, but not *too* personal. She learned his preference in music depended on his mood, that he loved

Italian dishes, played a decent but unremarkable round of golf, and gravitated toward Civil War history books. He kept abreast of politics, championed the underdog in sports, and was happy with his own company on most occasions.

By the end of the evening, when they were sitting on the deck and watching the sun set behind the row of thirty-year-old oak trees, she felt as if she knew what made him tick. At least she knew to a point, because no matter what he divulged she sensed there was a line in their conversation that he wouldn't cross.

A wise woman would allow a man his secrets, but his, she decided, were the destructive sort. Until he faced whatever had sent him fleeing St. Louis in the first place, he'd always be running.

Tonight, however, wasn't a night for unpleasant subjects. The gentle hush that slowly descended with the darkness, and the soothing sound of nature and the sweet scent of lilac hanging on the warm breeze only heightened her awareness of the man seated in the lounge chair beside hers.

"Would you like some coffee?" she asked. "It'll only take a minute to perk."

"No, thanks. It's getting late and I should be going. I have a colleague who stays up half the night, so one of us needs to be alert tomorrow."

She chuckled. "I'm crossing my fingers for a peaceful shift."

"I hope it works. Frankly, I'm surprised it's been quiet this long."

"I'm not. It's usually after midnight when parents decide their child can't wait until morning to be seen," she said wryly. "I'm safe for several more hours."

"In that case I'd better leave so you have time to yourself." He rose.

"I suppose," she said, reluctantly rising as his logic warred with her wishes.

He grabbed her hand. "Thanks again for dinner. It was delicious. My compliments to the chef."

"You're welcome."

He stroked her fingers, then pulled her close in order to hold her palm against his chest. "I haven't had an evening like this for quite some time." His voice was husky.

Her own breath caught in her throat. "Same for me. I—"

She didn't finish her sentence. In fact, as soon as his lips touched hers she forgot what she'd intended to say. Caught up in the moment, she stood on tiptoe and slipped her arms around his neck.

"I've wanted to do this ever since I tasted you last night," he murmured against her mouth. "I could hardly sleep, thinking about what it would be like."

"Now you don't have to think," she answered breathlessly. "You'll know."

Her words seemed to break through his hesitation. He moved his hands from her waist to her spine, and pressed her close as he deepened his kiss.

Instantly she felt the proof of his attraction—the proof that this wasn't a platonic response but one that signaled he wanted her. She'd never been the type to take the physical side of a relationship lightly, but somehow, even though she'd known him less than a week, it seemed as if she'd known him forever.

His tongue teased her mouth before slipping inside her parted lips. His exploration was foreign, and yet natural. Overwhelmed by the sensations he was creating, she felt her knees wobble and her toes curl in her sandals.

This was perfect. *He* was perfect.

Caught up in his embrace, it took her a minute to realize

his gentle assault had stopped. Another minute later he withdrew a fraction of a step, so that the night air could swirl between their bodies.

"I want you," he said hoarsely. "If circumstances were different…"

Instinctively she knew he referred to his personal life in general, not the current moment, when she was on call and neighbors would notice if his vehicle remained in her driveway past an acceptable hour. "Tell me about them," she said softly. "Maybe I can help."

He stroked the side of her face. "This is my journey, not yours."

"It doesn't matter," she insisted. "Whatever is bothering you—"

"Is my problem to solve. But if there *was* someone I wanted to talk to, it would be you." He dropped his hand, and his voice switched from a soft, tender tone to a harsher, more abrupt note. "Thanks again for a great evening."

"My pleasure." She followed him through the house, hating to have lost the special bond they'd started to create. "Just remember my door is always open and my ear is always ready to listen."

His smile was faint. "I won't forget."

As Ethan headed out of town, his engine purring like a well-fed cat, he gripped the steering wheel and cursed. Ivy's kiss and her sweet response had energized him to the point where he needed a long, brisk hike followed by an icy cold shower. Maybe then he'd be able to push aside the memories of Ivy's warm arms and soft curves.

He wanted her as much as he wanted air, but he'd truly be the worst sort of lowlife to take what she offered so generously and unreservedly and give her nothing in return.

Perhaps he should retrace his route and tell her his story. Perhaps she wouldn't blame him for his son's death like Tiffany had. On the other hand, being a medical professional herself, she might hold him even more responsible. She might have figured out that he was running from himself, but he'd rather not share the gritty details. Burying the past, not talking about it, was the only way to forget.

However, as he crawled into his lonely bed an hour and a cold shower later, he discovered that Ivy's softness, her fragrance, the way she made those little noises in her throat when he kissed her, were all indelibly etched in his memory.

Sheer desperation drove him to watch late-night television—although he couldn't recall any of the programming.

When his eyes felt gritty he finally fell asleep, dreaming of Ivy in his arms.

"Where's Ethan?" Ivy asked Heather midmorning the next day. Although she'd seen him when he arrived, looking as sharp as he always did, she knew him well enough now to notice the shadows under his eyes, as if he, too, had spent a relatively sleepless night. But after they'd greeted each other he'd retreated to his side of the hallway like a boxer returning to his corner.

At first she'd been hurt by his obvious rejection. Then she'd decided he was simply retreating until he gathered his courage to face her. No doubt he'd felt exposed and vulnerable last night, and this was his way of regaining control of the situation.

In a few minutes, though, he wouldn't be able to avoid her in order to lick his wounds.

"He went to E.R. Why? Are you curious, or did you need him for something?"

"I have a patient I want him to see right away," she said.

"He's been gone for almost thirty minutes, so I wouldn't think he'd be much longer," Heather answered. "Shall I tell him you're looking for him?"

"Yes, and if he's not back within five minutes, page him."

The nurse frowned. "Problems?"

"Possibly. I need his opinion on the Jantzen baby."

Heather eyed her. "You're going to ask him to examine an infant? After he's made it clear that the two don't mix?"

"He'll do it," she said, with more confidence than she felt.

"If you say so." The nurse sounded dubious. "Then again, if he helped out at the diner the other night, who knows what he'll do if you ask?" She snickered. "Is it true he kissed you in front of everyone?"

Ivy's face warmed. "It was a very small, very short kiss. Don't imagine motives that aren't there." Heaven help her if Heather or anyone else in town knew of their kiss last night, in the privacy of her home.

"If you say so, boss. But rumors about you two are flying."

Ivy groaned. "I was afraid of that."

"Why? You're both single. What did you think would happen? If you ask me, he's a real gem, and if you were smart, you'd do whatever you could to convince him to stay." She winked. "If I were in your shoes, I certainly would."

If only it were a matter of persuasion, but it wasn't. Ethan had secrets and fought demons that Ivy could only guess at, although she suspected it involved a patient. Maybe several. But, whatever it was, until he came to terms with his past she could talk until she turned blue and he wouldn't listen.

"You're not in my shoes, though." Then her mental thought about turning blue caused her to glance impatiently at her watch. "Call the E.R., and if no one's bleeding, he needs to be here now."

"I'll get right on it."

* * *

"Here are your X-rays, Doctor," the radiology technician said breathlessly as she rushed up to the E.R. nurses' station with a large envelope in hand. "I'm sorry for the delay."

He raised one eyebrow, restraining himself from delivering a caustic remark. It wasn't the girl's fault her processor had developed a glitch, thereby taking longer to develop the films than usual, but he hated waiting. Today, however, he managed to be halfway patient—mainly because his strategy for the day was to avoid Ivy. After dreaming of her last night, he couldn't guarantee that he wouldn't do something crazy, like drag her into an exam room and take up where they'd left off. Physical distance was the key, he'd decided.

So when the call had come in about a teenage patient arriving in the E.R. with a sports injury, he'd practically sprinted through the halls as fast as a fellow about to miss his flight.

Unfortunately avoiding Ivy had come with a price. He'd been forced to hang out in the empty E.R., counting the ceiling and floor tiles to pass the time. Now, though, with films in hand, his good humor returned—along with Nancy, the nurse who'd disappeared to locate a newspaper for him to read.

"Thanks." He pulled one of the films out of the manila envelope and held it over his head toward the fluorescent light in order to scrutinize the image. Seeing what he'd expected to see, he slid the film back inside its protective sleeve.

"I'll need a sling and a clavicle wrap, or a four-inch elastic bandage," he told her, before he strode back into Jason Sommerset's cubicle.

"I have good news and bad news," he told young Jason and his mother, Jane, as he immediately slid the films into the wall-mounted viewer and flicked on the light switch. "The bad news is that Jason has what I suspected from his symptoms. He has a broken collarbone—or clavicle, if you want the more technical term. You can see it quite plainly right here." He pointed to the area. "The good news is that he has very limited displacement of the bone, so we plan to keep it that way so it can heal. As soon as Nancy brings in my supplies—" The door opened and the nurse appeared with his requested items in her hands. "Ah, here she is. I'm going to immobilize his shoulder. You'll have to wear this, as well as a sling, for about four weeks."

Jason's hazel eyes sparkled. "Wow. No bath for a month!"

At Jane's look of horror, Ethan chuckled. "No such luck, sport. The strap you're getting will allow you to take it off and put it on yourself. Keep in mind that this doesn't mean you can take it off whenever you feel like it. It belongs on *you*, not your dresser, your bed, or on the floor, buried under dirty clothes— especially if you want to have unlimited activities in a month."

"OK. I can still play football, though, can't I?" he asked.

"After four weeks, I don't see why not," Ethan said.

Disappointment covered Jason's freckled face. "That's an awfully long time."

"Not really," Ethan said. "Look at the bright side. You'll still have plenty of summer left to do whatever you like. And by the time fall training begins you'll be in tip-top condition."

Jason's expression of relief was almost comical, but Ethan didn't laugh. Young teens were too self-conscious for him to do more than simply wink at Jason's mother.

"OK, then, sport. The sooner we get your shoulder taken care of, the sooner you can enjoy the rest of your day." Ethan began wrapping the figure-eight strap around Jason's shoulders and under his arms as he explained the process and showed the youth how to adjust the Velcro closures and foam shoulder pads.

"It needs to be tight, but not uncomfortable," he said, standing back to survey his handiwork. "How does that feel?"

Jason thought a minute, then nodded. "Fine."

"Good. Here's your sling." He placed it into position, so Jason could rest his left arm at the proper height.

"I gotta wear this, *too*?" Jason was aghast.

"Absolutely," Ethan said. "You don't want your arm to heal improperly, do you? Because if it does we may need more drastic measures like surgery to correct it. Then your recovery will definitely last into the football season."

Jason's eyes widened, as if that was an option he hadn't considered. Of course Ethan might have laid it on a bit thick, but sometimes the threat of worst-case scenario made the most recalcitrant patients compliant.

"I don't want that," Jason said fervently.

"Neither do I," Ethan said, and he stepped back once more. "Any tingling in your arm?"

"No."

Ethan checked Jason's radial pulse and hand skin color one last time. Both were normal, which indicated good blood flow. "Perfect. Now, if your shoulder aches—which I imagine it does—you may take acetaminophen or ibuprofen. Don't use aspirin, OK?"

Both Jason and Jane nodded.

"Go home and rest," Ethan advised his young patient. "If you have any problems or questions, call me. Otherwise make an appointment to see me—er, Dr. Ivy, in four weeks."

Ethan strode out of the cubicle and nearly mowed down Nancy. "Jason's all set," he informed her. "But if you would arrange for his follow-up appointment with Dr. Ivy's office before they leave, I'd appreciate it."

She nodded. "Your office just called. Dr. Ivy needs you asap."

"Did they say why?"

"No. Only that if no one was bleeding, you were to get back right away."

Once again he hustled back to the peds clinic, where he

found Ivy pacing the hall with a chart in her hand. She stopped as soon as she saw him.

"It's about time you got here," she said tartly.

Whatever it was must be serious, because he'd never seen Ivy look so worried. "I came as soon as I could. What's up?"

"I have a baby who—"

He held up both hands. "Wait a minute. I don't do babies, remember?"

"I know you don't, but I need a second opinion. You're the only one who can give me one."

Panic set in. "You don't want my opinion. If your gut gave you a preliminary diagnosis, then go with your instinct."

She grabbed his arm and tugged him inside the nearest room.

"I don't care if you think you don't know anything about babies, it doesn't matter. You're a *doctor*," she ground out. "And I need you to listen to this kid's chest and tell me what you hear. That's all."

He hesitated. Hearts and lungs worked the same, regardless of age and size. "How old is your patient?"

"Four months."

"This wasn't part of our arrangement," he reminded her, mentally screaming *this wasn't supposed to happen!*

She stiffened. "No, it wasn't. But sometimes allowances have to be made. This is one of them."

He hesitated and dug his suddenly sweaty hands inside his trouser pockets.

"Are you refusing to consult on a patient, Dr. Locke?" she asked crisply.

Although every fiber of his being demanded he refuse, he couldn't. He'd never be able to face Ivy, much less look himself in the eye, if he did.

"No," he said, surrendering unhappily. "I'll see him."

CHAPTER EIGHT

Ivy didn't understand why Ethan was so adamantly opposed to examining babies, but before the day ended she'd find out, she decided grimly. At the moment, though, she had to focus on her tiny patient.

She adjusted the chart that she'd tucked under one arm with a trembling hand. It would take a few minutes for relief to override the outrage still coursing through her veins, because she didn't know what she would have said or done if he'd walked away from her. But she was certain of one thing—her reaction wouldn't have been a pretty sight for anyone to behold.

"Good," she said, although the victory felt hollow. "Slade Jantzen had a regular check-up several weeks ago at another facility. His mother says it was unremarkable. Today she brought him in because she thinks he has a bluish cast to his skin whenever he eats or cries, and at times he seems to have trouble breathing. She wanted me to check him out."

"Pneumonia?"

"Not that I can tell," she admitted. "His lungs sound clear. Nothing."

"Did you order a chest X-ray?"

"Yes, but I haven't got the films yet. Radiology's processor is—"

"Having technical difficulties," he finished. "Yes, I know. What about his oxygen saturation?"

"It's low."

His face appeared grim, as if he were steeling himself for the moments ahead. "All right. Let's have a look at him."

Ivy led the way, introducing Ethan to Slade Jantzen's mother, Ginny, who was in her early thirties and nicely dressed. "He's going to examine Slade, too, because we want to be sure we don't miss anything," she told the other woman.

"Fine with me." Ginny placed her son on the baby exam table and took off his small shirt while Ethan and Ivy stood nearby. Slade wrinkled up his nose, waved his arms and grunted if he were about to protest the indignity of being undressed, but as soon the neckline cleared his head he settled down to a mild fussiness as he lay on the paper-lined surface.

Ivy drew Ginny off to one side of the table, where they would remain out of Ethan's way, yet she'd be close enough to observe Ethan's body language and assist if necessary. "Have you noticed anything else that might help us understand what's going on with your son?"

"Not really." Ginny wrung her hands as a worried wrinkle formed between her eyebrows. "Nothing specific I can put my finger on. But he just doesn't seem as active as my daughters were at this age. Slade seems content to watch what goes on rather than participate. He's never been a good eater, but it seems to be getting worse. He also seems fussier than he did when we brought him home. That could just be a difference in children's temperament, couldn't it?" She sounded as if she suspected something were wrong, but wanted to be convinced her son was healthy.

"It could be," Ivy said, unwilling to jump to conclusions, although the baby's cyanotic bouts weren't normal. "We may have to run a few more tests after Dr. Ethan is finished."

Ivy watched Ethan touch the baby, tentatively at first, his features appearing as chiseled and as cold as a statue's. She wondered with a sinking heart if she'd made a mistake when she'd pushed Ethan into his current position.

Suddenly, to her surprise, he drew a deep breath, glanced at her with an inscrutable gaze, paused for a millisecond, then handled the child like a pro. He listened to the little boy's chest, tickled his neck under his chin to bring a smile, expertly looked in his eyes, ears and mouth, and down his throat, and felt his abdomen. His large hands gently probed as he spoke words of encouragement to the small boy. Efficiently, he rolled Slade onto his stomach and waited, as if testing the baby's reaction to his new position.

Slade squirmed a bit, as if he didn't enjoy being on his tummy, but didn't make any large protest or attempt to voice his displeasure. Ivy knew a normal baby at his age would be trying to raise his head and chest, kicking and stretching and wriggling.

Ethan rolled Slade back onto his back, then placed him in a sitting position before he listened to his heart once again. Ivy watched carefully, hoping Ethan would hear what she had and confirm her suspicions. Yes, she could have immediately sent the baby to a specialist, but she was conscious of the expense, and she didn't want to "cry wolf" if there was a simple explanation.

A minute later Ethan unhooked the stethoscope from his ears in an adept one-handed motion and wore it like a necklace so that Slade could play with the chestpiece dangling near him.

The baby obliged. He swatted the rubber tubing as if trying to grab it. Ethan smiled, looking far more at ease as he stroked down several spiked strands of Slade's fine blond hair.

At that moment Ivy knew Ethan Locke was a fraud. Babies

were his forte, because he handled this one as easily as a surgeon wielded a scalpel. The next question was, *why did he deny his ability?*

"Slade's lungs sound great," Ethan admitted as he rubbed the baby's back a final time before picking him up and handing him to his mother. "I did pick up a heart murmur," he said, sending a meaningful glance at Ivy.

Although relieved he'd confirmed her clinical observation, she was certain he saw the residual question in her eyes because he looked away.

"No one has ever told me that before," Ginny exclaimed. "The last doctor said everything sounded fine."

"A heart murmur is just an extra or an unusual noise," he explained. "It could be harmless, or a sign of an abnormality. Considering his age, and the fact that no one's discovered it before, and that he has episodes when he's cyanotic or looks blue, we should run a few tests."

"What tests?" Ginny paused from tugging Slade's shirt over his head to ask.

"An ECG," Ivy interjected. "An electrocardiogram. It'll be quick and painless."

"If Dr. Ivy hasn't ordered lab work yet, we'll run a blood count to get an idea of his hemoglobin and red blood cell numbers," Ethan added. "The red cells carry hemoglobin, which carries the oxygen to his tissues. If he's not getting enough oxygen because he's anemic or for some other reason—"

"He turns blue," Ginny finished. She hoisted Slade onto her shoulder and patted his back to ease his obvious fussiness.

Ethan nodded. "Exactly. After we get those results we'll have a better idea of what is going on with your son."

"I'll make the arrangements," Ivy told Ginny. "As soon as they've drawn Slade's blood sample and done the EKG come back here. We should have a few answers in an hour or so, if you want to phone your husband."

"Thanks. I'll call him."

By the time Ivy turned to leave the cubicle Ethan had gone. She was tempted to find him, but her questions could wait. Slade was her top priority, and if her instincts were correct Ethan wasn't in a talkative frame of mind anyway.

As she'd predicted to Ginny, she had the lab reports, ECG tracing and chest films in her hands within the hour. Armed with information, and determined to shelve her curiosity for the moment, she found Ethan in the lounge, clutching his coffee mug with both hands and staring moodily into the cup.

"Here are Slade's reports," she said, placing them on the table.

"And?" He reached for the top one.

"His RBC and hemoglobin levels are above normal for a child his age. His lungs on the X-ray look OK, and I can't say his heart looks grossly abnormal, but I'm not a radiologist," she admitted.

He pulled out the chest films and held them up to the overhead light, one at a time. "His heart seems small and he has a right aortic arch. The main pulmonary artery segment almost appears concave. See how this area is curved inward slightly?" He pointed to the location. "But it's hard to tell for certain from these particular films."

For a man who refused to deal with babies, he seemed well versed in reading their X-rays, and she said so.

"Not now, Ivy," he said tiredly.

"Then when?"

"I don't know…later. What else do you have?"

She recognized his diversion tactic, but it was necessary. The patient should be her main concern at this moment, not Ethan's past.

"His ECG is definitely abnormal." She shifted pages to produce the tracing. "From the longer P waves, taller R and shorter S waves, he has something going on with his right ventricle."

"And when you add in the systolic-ejection murmur, you have a child with a serious heart defect," Ethan finished.

"That's what I was afraid of," Ivy said ruefully, "but I wanted a second opinion."

"In fact, I'm guessing young Slade has Tet," he said, using the shorthand for a condition known as Tetralogy of Fallot. This congenital defect involved four abnormalities of the heart and, given this baby's problems, would require surgery to correct. "You can't keep him here."

As if she needed Ethan to point out the obvious. "I know. I'll tell his parents."

Heather burst into the room. "Someone needs to come asap. The Jantzen baby is turning blue."

Ivy took off, aware of Ethan on her heels as she burst into the cubicle where young Slade was crying and struggling for air. His parents tried to soothe their son, but they weren't succeeding. Instead, they looked at Ivy helplessly.

"We need oxygen," she informed Heather, as Ethan grabbed the baby from his mother and placed him on his back on the exam table.

"What's wrong?" Ginny cried, clutching her husband's arm for support.

"We believe he has a heart defect," Ivy said, watching as Ethan pushed the baby's knees to his little chest. A minute later Heather wheeled in a small tank of oxygen. While Ethan fitted a pediatric-sized mask over Slade's face, Ivy heard his calm request for morphine.

In the back of her mind she wanted to believe his swift and focused actions were evidence of a phenomenal memory for his med-school pediatric training, but in her heart she knew the evidence she saw was indisputable. He'd done this procedure often enough for it to become second nature.

What else hadn't he told her?

More importantly, why hadn't he trusted her?

Anger and hurt suddenly flared, high enough to drown out her earlier curiosity.

"A heart defect?"

Slade's father's comment pulled her back to the conversation at hand, and she struggled to maintain an even tone. "I can't say exactly, because he needs more sophisticated tests than we have available," she said honestly, unwilling to share their diagnosis of Tet without all the supporting evidence. "But what's happening is that the oxygen-poor blood coming into the heart is mixing with the oxygen-rich blood leaving the heart. Normally the heart's system of valves doesn't allow that to happen."

"So what do we do?"

"I'll call the air ambulance, as well as a pediatric cardiac surgeon," she said decisively. "He'll run more tests, especially a noninvasive echocardiogram, where sound waves will give him a picture of the heart's structure. As soon as he determines what's wrong he'll take him to surgery and correct the problem."

Ginny's chin quivered and her eyes glistened as she sniffled. "Surgery?"

"They have remarkable success these days," Ivy assured her. "It's his only chance to have a normal life."

Mr. Jantzen gripped his wife's hand. "We understand."

Ginny addressed Ethan. "Why are you holding his knees to his chest, and what did you give him?"

He met the woman's gaze as he held Slade in position with one large but gently soothing hand. "Placing him in this position increases pressure in his aorta and the left side of his heart, and ultimately improves circulation to the lungs. We gave him morphine because it decreases the severity of his spells. These are only temporary solutions to keep him stable until he's under a cardiac specialist's care."

Ivy noticed Slade's skin color had pinkened considerably. "We'll take him to the E.R. now, while we wait for transport. But don't worry," she told the couple kindly. "Someone will be with you and Slade at all times. In fact, I'm sure he'd appreciate having his mommy carry him."

She spoke to Ethan, hating that the temperature of her voice had cooled several degrees, but she couldn't pretend to be friendly when she felt so betrayed and used. "Will you go with them while I make the arrangements?"

His forehead wrinkled and his eyes reflected the same haunting shadows she'd seen that one night in the diner. He started to shake his head, then stopped, as if he were reconsidering.

"Yeah. I'll go," he finally murmured.

Ivy turned back to the couple. "I'll catch up to you in the E.R. And don't worry. Slade is in good hands. Dr. Ethan knows what he's doing in situations like these."

The tension on the Jantzens' faces eased with her endorsement, but Ethan froze. He clearly hadn't expected to receive such a glowing reference, yet in spite of his lie of omission, in spite of her feelings of betrayal, she had confidence in his abilities. It seemed important to tell him so.

As he'd promised, Ethan remained with Slade while Ivy contacted the air ambulance service and a pediatric cardiologist, who gave her the same instructions that Ethan had already implemented.

He took her news in stride as they each steered their conversation along politely professional lines, without their usual easy banter. Other than speaking when absolutely necessary Ethan had withdrawn—probably to prepare himself for the accounting she would demand when the opportunity presented itself.

An hour later the helicopter arrived, with a nurse practitioner and an E.M.T. who took charge with Ivy's blessing. Shortly after young Slade was taking his first chopper ride, and shortly after that Ivy had returned to the relative quiet of her practice.

As much as she wanted to corner Ethan, she knew she had to bide her time. This discussion required privacy and no interruptions.

After Ivy had seen her last patient and the office was empty, by four-thirty, she was ready to make her move. Unfortunately he had disappeared.

"You just missed him," her receptionist told her apologetically. "He didn't have any more appointments so he decided to leave early. If I'd known you wanted him to stay, I would have—"

"It's okay. I just had a question for him. Nothing that can't wait until later," she lied. "Did he say where he was going?"

"No. I didn't ask and he didn't offer."

Considering it was far too early to eat dinner, although they'd missed lunch because of little Slade Jantzen, Ivy doubted she'd find him at the diner. He'd probably gone home to lick his wounds in private.

She was determined not to let him.

Ivy hurried down the connecting hallway that led to Walt's office, where she found both Jed and Walt's nurse practitioner behind a stack of charts on their desks.

"I have a favor to ask, Margery," Ivy said. "I'll buy, beg, borrow or steal whatever it takes for you to say yes."

The forty-five-year-old Margery laughed. "Sounds like a deal. What do you need?"

Ivy explained, her fingers crossed. Although she'd manage somehow if Margery couldn't help her, it would make life so much simpler if she did.

"Sure—no problem," the N.P. said.

Grateful, Ivy flew home. She changed into a sleeveless blouse and comfortable shorts, dug a pizza out of her freezer, grabbed a six-pack of sugar-laden caffeinated soda pop, then headed for Ethan's cabin.

Her car ate up the miles and she told herself to remain calm. Although as the moment of truth loomed ahead of her a familiar sense of pain surfaced. She didn't know if it was for Ethan or for herself.

The more she thought about her feelings, the more she realized it was ridiculous to feel hurt and betrayed. She'd only met the man a mere five days ago! As she reminded herself of that, she knew time had nothing to do with the strength of her feelings. After the kisses they'd shared, their companionship, his thoughtful gestures, he should have trusted her with his secrets. And yet he hadn't.

Her righteous indignation lasted until he answered her brisk knock and she saw his bleak face. Her own hurts hadn't disappeared, but now they seemed small and insignificant in comparison to the private war still waging inside of him.

Ethan had been expecting to hear from Ivy, but he'd been waiting for the telephone to ring instead of a personal appearance. Sending her packing when she stood on his doorstep would be more difficult than disconnecting a call.

"Hi," she said quietly. "You left early today."

He raised a sardonic eyebrow before he drank from the bottle of beer in his hand. "Feel free to dock my salary for the hour."

She raised the box in her hand. "I brought pizza."

"I'm not hungry."

"It'll keep." She paused. "May I come in?"

He didn't want company. He wanted hers least of all. "I don't suppose you'll go home if I say no."

"Not a chance. I'll camp out here on the sidewalk until you agree." Her tone softened. "You need to talk, Ethan."

She was right, he thought wearily, but when he did Ivy would see him in a completely different light and the acceptance in her eyes would fade.

"Fine," he retorted, heading away from the door and forgoing the gentlemanly ritual of holding it for her. "Come in."

He finished his bottle, tossed it in the trash can and forced himself to retrieve a plastic bottle of water instead of a second beer from the refrigerator. As tempting as it was to drown his sorrows, trying to do so on the two bottles of beer in his refrigerator was impossible. He'd also learned long ago that drinking himself into oblivion only added a monstrous hangover to his woes and wasn't worth the few hours of forgetfulness.

He broke the seal, sank onto the sofa, and rested his sock-clad feet on the coffee table while Ivy slipped the pizza into his freezer, presumably for later.

Out of the corner of his eye he watched her sink gracefully into the easy chair on his right. He tried to read her mood, but couldn't. This Ivy was far more serious and pensive than the one he'd come to know, but at least she wasn't angry.

He hadn't intended to hurt her, but he had. He should have kept their relationship purely professional, but she'd been like a long drink of cool water on a hot, sunny day and he hadn't been able to stay away.

His idea that he could separate his past from his present under carefully guarded conditions had been faulty. Once again he'd pay the price for his decision, but he wasn't in a hurry to do so.

"Any word on the Jantzen boy?" he asked.

"Not yet. I'm going to call in a few hours for an update." She hesitated. "Why did you lead me to believe you didn't have experience with infants?"

"It was easier than telling the truth."

"Which is?"

"I am—er *was* a neonatologist. I was on the fast track to becoming head of department when my boss retired in a few years, but I gave it up and left St. Louis in search of the peace I couldn't find there."

He studied the brick pattern on the fireplace to avoid her gaze, although he sensed she was studying him intently.

"What happened?" she prompted.

"Do you remember the first morning we met? You asked me if I had any children. I don't, but I did. His name was Cody Alan Locke. He died six weeks after he was born."

"I'm so sorry, Ethan."

He ignored her condolences. He'd heard them so often they no longer meant anything. How could she or anyone else imagine or know the pain he'd felt?

"His mother and I had a long engagement. Her pregnancy came as a surprise, but she wanted to wait to hold the ceremony until after the baby was born. Rushing the wedding and walking down the aisle in a maternity gown didn't sit well with her, so I gave in. At twenty-six weeks she went into premature labor and her OB-GYN couldn't stop it. Cody was born and whisked up to my NICU, where he immediately had problems with his blood sugar. We fought a constant battle against hypoglycemia."

"PHHI?" she asked.

"Yes," he said. Those were letters he'd come to hate. Persistent Hyperinsulinemic Hypoglycemia of Infancy. A complicated condition with a long-winded name for such a tiny scrap of humanity. "His insulin levels were high and his glucose levels low, and we tried everything to even the score. Several of the consultants recommended surgery to remove part or most of his pancreas, depending on what the pathologist found on the biopsies, but I was confident that the next drug or a new dosage would magically control the problem. I was wrong. By the time I agreed to surgery he couldn't handle the procedure. He died on the table."

Ivy wanted to wrap her arms around him, but he was too caught up in his memories to appreciate her gesture. After hearing his story, she now understood the reason for the shadows in his eyes.

"So you gave up medicine?"

"Not then," he said. "I didn't make that decision until later. A few weeks after Cody died Tiffany left me. She said I was responsible for his death and she couldn't bear to be around me. I didn't blame her. I couldn't bear to be around myself."

Ivy considered his former fiancée with disgust, but held back her comments. Ethan was finally talking, and she didn't want to interrupt.

"Losing her was another blow, but I weathered it," he said. "Barely. The last straw broke after I lost another neonate to necrotizing enterocolitis. By then I admitted I had lost my edge and it was time to step aside. So I did. I left St. Louis with the belief I'd find a new career on my extended vacation. Something where I wouldn't have to make life-and-death decisions."

"And you ended up in Danton," she murmured.

"Yeah." He glanced at her with pain-filled eyes. "I never intended to go back into medicine. I should have held my ground after you visited that first day, but I felt guilty because I remembered what it was like to work when I was dead on my feet. In the end I was damned if I did and damned if I didn't," he finished ruefully.

"So you set your conditions in order to protect yourself?"

He nodded. "It worked, too. Until today."

"I wish you had told me."

"I couldn't. I was afraid I'd see the same disgust in your eyes that I saw in Tiffany's. You made me feel like I could believe in myself again, and I couldn't risk losing that."

Her heart pounded. "Oh, Ethan," she said. "I wish I'd known. I might have handled things differently with the Jantzen baby."

"Maybe. Maybe not. If you hadn't asked for a consult today, you would have at some point. It was inevitable." He leaned against the back cushions and drank deeply from his water bottle. "Now you know the sordid details. If you don't want me to come in on Monday, you won't hurt my feelings. I'll understand."

She hated seeing his defeated attitude, but sensed that if she sympathized with him, he'd never get past it. "If you think I'm letting you off the hook this easily you'd better think twice," she said tartly. "You promised to help me for three weeks, and by my calendar I still have two weeks to go."

Surprise flitted across his face. "After what I just told you—you still want me to treat your patients?"

"Why wouldn't I?" she asked, certain he'd continue to wallow in self-doubt if she didn't give him a dose of tough love. "For the record, I don't believe you were responsible for your son's death." At his protest, she cut him off. "You weren't the doctor-of-record, were you?"

"No," he said slowly. "My boss, Stewart, was. But—"

"Then it was Stewart's responsibility to convince you to take other treatment alternatives. Barring that, he could always have pressed the issue and gone the legal route if you'd refused to follow his advice. He didn't, so that tells me he was content, at least to some degree, with your decision." She softened her tone. "I'm sorry your son died, Ethan, but no matter how hard we wish it, or how hard we try, we aren't God. Some things are out of our hands. If you want my opinion, your fiancée was wrong to blame you when you were trying to save your son's life. Unfortunately, bad things happen. Period. I hope she learns that someday. As for your last case, NEC is something the bedside nurse usually notices first. Did you ignore her reports?"

"No. I ran tests, but they didn't show anything specific. Sometimes infants with feeding issues show the same symptoms, so we waited and watched. Just when we thought the baby was in the clear the bowel perforated, and we couldn't get her to surgery fast enough."

"Ethan," she said kindly, moving to sit beside him on the sofa and cradle his hand in hers, "you did what you could. You probably did what any of your colleagues would have done and I'll bet they told you that."

"They did."

"Then let it go. It's time."

He paused.

She leaned over and kissed him, softly at first, but it steadily grew into a heated expression of what lay in her heart.

Ethan didn't move until suddenly he flung an arm around her shoulders and drew her close. "Ivy," he whispered against her mouth. "I was so afraid—"

"Don't be," she replied.

"I should tell you something else."

She could barely string two thoughts together under the sensation of his mouth trailing down her neck. "What?"

"I've wanted you from the day we met."

In some functioning portion of her brain she recognized the proof of his desire. What would making love with the man who had sneaked into her heart be like? The prospect of finding out for herself sent her heart into racing mode. There was nothing in this world that she wanted more. Nothing in this world felt more perfect.

To her consternation, he slowly turned down the heat until he'd put space between them. His eyes, his expression, revealed regret and apology. "You know I want this, don't you?"

"I want it, too. So why—?"

"I can't. As right as it seems, I can't make love to you when I'll be leaving in a few weeks."

"You could stay."

His smile was small. "It's tempting."

In her heart, though, she knew he wouldn't yield easily. His war within still waged too strong for him to believe he deserved his own happy ending. As much as she wanted him to remain, and would do everything in her power to convince him, she also wanted him to stay for the right reasons. Running away from St. Louis so he could hide from his fears wasn't one of them.

"Then I'll keep working on it," she promised. "But no matter what you decide about the future, please make love to me now, Ethan. It's what we both want."

He ran one hand through his hair, his indecision plain as he wrestled with his desires. "Don't make this so difficult," he said hoarsely. "I'm trying to do the right thing."

She rested her fingers on his forearm. "I appreciate the considerate gesture, but it isn't necessary."

His uncertainty faded and a cautious hope filled his eyes. "You're certain?"

"Very."

"I don't want you to have regrets," he warned.

"Please don't make me beg, Ethan. The only regret I'll have is if we *don't* do this."

He jumped to his feet and began to pace. Certain he was putting distance between them, she felt rejection spear her soul. But before her hopes completely drained out of the hole he'd created, he turned around to reach out, grab her hand and tug her upright.

"Me, too," he said in a husky voice. "I've lived with enough regrets. I don't want to add to the list."

Happiness soared through her and she slipped her arms around his waist. "Neither do I." Stretching on her toes, she pressed her lips to his in a kiss packed with emotion.

Once again, he broke contact. "No."

Impatience reared its head. "No? After that you've said *no*?" Her voice raised.

He grinned like a mischievous little boy. "I'm objecting to the location, not the activity." He quickly ushered her down the hallway. "I won't make love on the sofa like a teenager."

Eager to have him to herself, because these few seconds' delay was killing her, she said, "I don't mind."

"I do," he said firmly. "If you want the sofa, we can try it later, but not the first time."

Anticipation tingled down her spine as his words soaked into her feverish brain. My, oh, my, but she loved the way this man thought.

CHAPTER NINE

THEY'D barely crossed the threshold to his bedroom when Ethan's mouth met hers and his hands began a careful exploration that drove her out of her mind. She mumbled her impatience.

"You don't want slow and easy?" he murmured as he eased a shirt button through its hole.

"Later," she said breathlessly. "Not the first time."

"Turning my own words against me, are you?" Another button eased free.

"Yes." She tugged his polo shirt out of his waistband and slipped her hands underneath. Her palms glided along his chest and her fingertips encountered tight abs and a sprinkling of coarse hair.

"In that case…" The last few buttons slipped from their mooring as if by magic, and he peeled her blouse off her shoulders in one smooth motion. His knuckles grazed the upper swell of her breasts before he parted her bra and flung it somewhere on the floor.

His hands roamed, cupped and teased her flesh, and she moaned her pleasure. In the wink of an eye the rest of her clothing vanished, and she was lying on top of a satiny coverlet that cooled her skin.

Before she could register anything else he loomed over her, completely and gloriously free of his own garments.

He was a vision she would never forget. Muscles bulged in his arms as he lowered himself to fit her body against his. His fingers mapped trails all over her body until she thought she'd burst into flames. His featherlight touch turned her into a quivering mass. But he wasn't finished.

He rained kisses on her mouth before traveling down the side of her neck, across her shoulders, through the valley of her breasts and coming to a stop at her navel. Waves of sensation crashed through her, and she writhed under his gentle yet unrelenting attack.

Anchoring her close, he reached to the bedside table and groped inside a drawer. When he fumbled with the packet he'd retrieved, and cursed under his breath, she smiled. For a man whose hands could do the most beautiful things, evoke the most delightful sensations, being bested by a small foil pouch made her think that he didn't engage in making love precipitately.

"Let me," she said.

With a huff of disgust he handed over the goods and she took care of the details.

He grabbed her wrist as she finished. "As good as your hands feel, I don't want this to be over before it's started."

His admonition made her feel powerful, but the tables soon turned when he took up where he'd left off. Then, as if his instincts were so attuned to her body's response that he knew she couldn't bear to wait another minute, he slid inside her.

He paused briefly to allow her to adjust to his size before he began to move. Slow, even strokes became a steady rhythm that drove her into a state where passion reigned supreme and everything else faded into insignificance.

This was what she wanted, she managed to think, before

Ethan drove her completely over the edge into a freefall that seemed timeless.

Finally they both relaxed in each other's embrace. No matter what the days ahead brought, whether Ethan remained or not, Ivy would treasure these moments.

"You're beautiful," he whispered. "Inside and out."

"Thank you," she answered, enjoying his warmth as they lay nestled together.

"Comfortable?" he asked.

"Perfectly."

"Good, because I don't think I can move."

Pleased she'd affected him so strongly, she grinned as she raised herself on one elbow to stare into his face and trace circles on his broad chest. "Maybe I should throw that pizza in the oven so you can get your strength back?"

In one swift motion he maneuvered her so she was lying flat underneath him. "Later," he said. "Pizza sounds good, but I'm hungrier for you."

"Really?"

"Yes, really." He gazed at her with enough longing to prove he hadn't exaggerated. Yet what struck her the most was that the shadows she'd seen in his eyes had disappeared.

"You're right," she said. "Pizza can wait."

And it did—for a very long time.

"Are you sure we have to attend the rodeo?" Ethan asked the next day as he parked his car in the gravel parking lot outside the rodeo grounds. "I can think of more enjoyable ways to pass the afternoon than walking around a dusty fairground and getting sunburned."

Ivy laughed. "So can I. But we have to put in an appearance. With Margery taking call for me last night, if neither of us are seen today, we'll be gossip fodder."

The joys of living in a small-town fishbowl. He didn't mind for himself, but Ivy's reputation was a different story. She would live with the consequences of their actions for years, because people had long memories.

"I suppose." He hopped out of his vehicle and escorted Ivy through the uneven lot toward the fairground entrance, which was marked by colored balloons, a banner proclaiming "Thirty-Fifth Annual Danton Frontier Days Rodeo", and several clowns handing out folded pieces of paper.

"What would you like to see first?" she asked.

"I've never attended a rodeo," he admitted. "As far as I'm concerned this is your parade, so we'll do whatever you want." He leaned close to her ear. "As long as I can steal a kiss every now and then, I'll be happy."

Her melodic laugh touched his heartstrings. "I'll see what I can do."

As they approached the entrance, two clowns greeted them both by name and handed over the program of events.

"Enjoy yourself, Dr. Ethan," a clown told him, in a tone that belied his sad expression. "We're thrilled you could join in the festivities this weekend."

"Thanks. I am, too," he said, realizing he meant it.

"Great. Folks around here are pretty proud of our rodeo, so be sure you see everything."

"We will," he promised.

"And don't forget the food," the happy clown added. "Harvey's turkey legs are exceptional this year." He turned away to greet more newcomers. "Hello, folks. Welcome to the rodeo."

Ethan guided Ivy over the uneven ground with one hand at the small of her back. "I wonder if the turkey legs are better than the pizza we had last night?"

Her smile dazzled him. "Taste-wise, probably, but the ambience can't compare."

Making love on the sofa while they waited for the pizza to bake didn't come close to standing in line with a crowd of people, waiting for a deep-fat-fried drumstick, no matter how delicious it was.

"Look," she said, pointing ahead. "There are the craft booths. I promised several people I'd stop at theirs. Do you mind?"

"Not at all." He glanced at the program. "The calf-roping is scheduled in a half-hour."

"You definitely have to see that. And when we're finished watching the events we can meander over to the carnival rides. The ferris wheel is my favorite."

Ethan followed her to the craft stalls, content to walk alongside her and watch. What surprised him, though, was how so many people stopped to visit with him.

Not with Ivy, with *him*. And these weren't only the familiar faces of hospital staff members, but were people he'd seen at the grocery store, the gas station and the diner. Nearly everyone called him by name as they smiled and waved.

A week ago he'd received an occasional polite nod, and now it was as if someone had declared him a new resident and placed his name on the tax rolls.

It bothered him, because he hadn't intended to befriend anyone. What was the point when he hadn't planned to stick around? In fact, he still didn't, although if he were truly honest, Danton wouldn't be a bad place to call the end of the road.

But was he ready to return to medicine full-time? And, if so, would it be as a general pediatrician or as a neonatologist?

His decision boiled down to one thing. *What did he want?*

He honestly didn't know.

Admittedly, he was enjoying his stint as Ivy's colleague more than he'd expected. He was still undecided as to whether his satisfaction was due to dabbling in medicine again or if Ivy had made the difference.

Regardless of the source of his current contentment, and in spite of Ivy's assurances, he wasn't ready to be responsible for preemies. Until then he simply couldn't reclaim his specialty career.

On the other hand, dealing with the older crowd was far different than handling neonates, and he didn't feel completely ready to do that, either. He'd been lucky so far and been able to switch gears, but he'd definitely have to bone up on topics that were non-issues for preemies. He didn't mind studying and learning, but, again, what did he want?

One thing, however, was clear. If he didn't embrace a medical career of some sort, he couldn't stay. Considering the need for doctors in Danton, how could he deny providing a service so desperately needed? He'd have to leave, even though it would mean leaving Ivy behind.

The only bright spot was that he didn't have to decide his future today. In the meantime he intended to savor his moments with Ivy and let tomorrow worry about itself.

"Did you have a good weekend?" Heather asked on Monday. "I saw you dragged Ethan to the rodeo."

Ivy grinned. The weekend had exceeded her expectations, but sharing that would put ideas into Heather's head, and her friend didn't need any help. "Ethan and I went together," she admitted. "We watched most of the events, rode a few rides, stuffed ourselves to the gills, and then went home."

Cuddling against Ethan as they rode the ferris wheel had been a real treat. Rather than perch the over-sized white teddy bear he'd won after buying countless attempts at the baseball toss between them on the seat, she'd buckled it in the corner, so that she could sit next to Ethan.

They'd sampled turkey legs, roasted corn on the cob,

cotton candy, funnel cakes and caramel apples until she'd thought she wouldn't be able to eat for an entire week.

The real treat had come when he'd taken her home as dusk fell. They'd shared a shower and made love until midnight, when reluctantly, after spending nearly thirty-six hours together, he'd driven back to his place.

Sunday, however, had been another day. Because she'd been on call, he'd driven into town, and they'd spent the afternoon together in undisturbed bliss. In fact, the weekend had been so free of interruptions Ivy had checked her pager numerous times to be sure the battery hadn't died.

"I'm glad you had a restful weekend," Heather said now. "I talked to Nancy and she said the hospital was quiet."

Ivy nodded. "I think everyone wanted to attend the rodeo, which suited me just fine."

"Which means we'll be swamped today, with sunburn, bug bites and upset stomachs from all the junk food," Heather said knowledgeably. "It happens every year."

This being her first summer, Ivy took her friend's word. At that moment, though, Heather could have told her the grass was purple and blue polka-dotted and she wouldn't have questioned her, because Ethan had walked in, looking remarkably handsome and tanned. Everything else faded into insignificance.

"Hi." She greeted him hoping she sounded as normal as she had last week. No one needed to know or guess that they'd become more than colleagues.

"Good morning," he said formally, although he winked at her.

"Now that you're both here," Heather said, apparently oblivious to the undercurrents swirling between them, "I see we have a lot of well-baby check-ups this morning, so I hope you won't mind if I shuffle some of the toddlers over to you, Dr. Ethan?"

Ivy met his gaze, uncertain of his response, but instead of objecting he simply nodded.

"That's fine," he told Heather, although he faced Ivy as if sending her a silent message. "In fact, if Ivy gets bogged down, let me know. I might be able to help a bit with the younger set."

Ivy was too stunned to reply, but she took his offer as a positive sign. Perhaps his experience on Friday and her confidence had made an impact on him. She hoped so.

But if his offer had rendered her speechless, it produced the opposite effect on Heather. "That's wonderful, but I thought—" She stopped, as if uncertain what to say next.

"It's been a long time since I worked with that age group," Ethan replied smoothly. "But after working with the Jantzen baby Ivy convinced me I can handle them."

"I saw you in action, so I'd agree," Heather said vehemently. "How is he doing, by the way?"

"I talked to his doctor on Saturday," Ivy answered. "He has Tetralogy of Fallot, as we suspected, and they're going to perform surgery to alleviate his symptoms until he's big enough for a complete repair. He's going to be fine."

"What a relief." Heather consulted the notepad she'd removed from her pocket. "If you two will excuse me, I have to restock a couple of rooms before the hordes descend. Can't have you guys running out of vinyl gloves or tongue depressors."

As soon as Heather had moved out of earshot, Ethan spoke to Ivy. "Do you have plans for this evening?"

Anticipation skipped down her spine. "No."

"How about dinner and a movie?" he asked. "I stopped at the grocery store this morning for a newspaper and a DVD caught my eye. I've been wanting to see it ever since it won an Academy Award last year."

She didn't care if he wanted to view a 1940s black-and-white film. Being together was more important to her than what they did, although certain activities—her face warmed as she imagined a few of them—came close.

"Sounds great."

"I'll rent a copy after work," he promised.

As he turned to leave, she stopped him. "You don't have to help with my little rug rats." She smiled as she referred fondly to her smallest patients. "I can handle them."

"I know, and I'm not horning in on your territory," he said. "But I want to share the full load, not just part of it. I need to do this, Ivy, so I'll know if I can."

"OK," she said with equanimity, although inside her emotions churned. She was proud of him for taking the first shaky step toward facing his fears, but if he chose to return to his former calling, what would it mean for them?

No regrets, she told herself. From the beginning she'd expected him to leave, and had resigned herself to it. Just because her heart had gotten involved and she'd fallen in love, she couldn't change the rules at this late date.

"Someone to see you, Dr. Ethan." On the following Thursday Heather interrupted him as he finished the notes on his last case.

Ethan groaned good-naturedly. "I thought you said we were done?"

"We are. The fellow waiting to see you in the lobby isn't a patient. He claims he's an old friend of yours."

"Thanks, Heather." Curious, Ethan headed toward the now-empty lobby. Although he'd been accepted in the community, and now knew a lot of the townsfolk by name, he didn't call anyone in particular a friend, much less an old one.

The mystery was solved as soon as he saw the tall, slightly graying man studying the Anne Geddes prints, much as Ethan had done two weeks ago.

"Stewart," Ethan said, thrilled to see his friend and former boss. "It's good to see you. What brings you to this neck of the woods?"

Stewart Trimble smiled as he clapped Ethan on the back. "I was heading to Oklahoma City for meetings, and after finding Danton on the map I decided to take a small detour. How've you been?"

In spite of his former superior's jovial attitude, Ethan felt Stewart's piercing gaze. "I'm fine," he said sincerely. "Just fine."

Apparently Stewart saw something in Ethan's demeanor that satisfied him, because he nodded and the concern in his eyes faded. "I can see that. To be honest, I'm surprised to find you in a doctors' office, of all places. When I asked the filling station attendant if he knew you and he sent me to the clinic, I was certain we were talking about two different people." He grinned. "I'm glad to see I was wrong."

"I'm rather surprised myself," Ethan admitted. "Ivy asked me to help her for a few weeks in her general peds practice even before you started hounding me to keep my hand in medicine, so I gave in. Come on. I'll show you around."

Ethan proudly escorted his mentor through their portion of the clinic, and they had just passed Ivy's office when she came round the corner, her expression pensive. "Ivy, I'd like you to meet Stewart Trimble."

Ivy shifted the stack of charts in her arms to shake his hand. "Pleased to meet you," she said warmly.

Ethan nodded. "Stew's my former boss."

Her smile wavered, although Ethan doubted if Stewart had noticed. *He* had only noticed because he'd learned to read Ivy as well as his copy of *Fundamentals of Pediatrics*. "You're a long way from home," she mentioned.

"I'm traveling through to Oklahoma City," Stewart explained, "and I thought I'd check on Ethan."

"Great," she replied, although her smile seemed shaky. "Would you like to stay for dinner?"

"I would, but I'm eager to find my hotel before dark," he said. "Maybe next time."

"Yes, maybe next time," she echoed.

Concerned by her preoccupied demeanor, Ethan asked. "Did you need me for anything?"

"No, not at all," she answered. "I had something to tell you, but it can wait." She addressed Stewart. "Have a safe trip," she said, before she headed down the hall toward the receptionist's desk.

"So that's your colleague." Stewart's gaze followed Ivy. "Married?"

Ethan grinned. "No."

Stewart chuckled. "Something tells me my so-called hounding didn't convince you to act as a locum in her practice."

"Not entirely," Ethan admitted, unwilling to define his relationship with Ivy to anyone, including his former boss. "But it didn't hurt," he finished.

"However she convinced you to rejoin society, I'm grateful," Stewart said simply. "You were on the fast track to nowhere."

How well Ethan knew that to be true. After working with Ivy for almost two weeks, he hadn't felt this contented for a long time. She'd accepted and embraced him, history and all, and had given him a freedom that he hadn't experienced since he'd heard his son's final prognosis. How ironic to think that one infant had turned his life upside down and another had figured prominently in restoring it. If Slade hadn't come in, and if Ivy hadn't insisted on a consultation, Ethan would still be locked in his no-win situation.

"I was," Ethan agreed. "But enough about me. How about a cup of coffee for the road?"

"I'd love one," Stewart said. "If the cinnamon I'm smelling is any indication, I'd say you've converted the staff just like you did at the children's hospital."

Ethan laughed as he showed him to a chair at the table in their tiny lounge and placed a mug of coffee in front of his guest. "I have."

"Another conquest to the world of gourmet coffee." Stewart's face lost its teasing expression and grew serious. "I think you know how worried we've been about you, Ethan."

"I do," he said simply. During the long weeks after the funeral, and after Tiffany had moved out of their house, Stewart had kept close tabs on him. "A single day didn't go by without you calling or dropping by to see me."

"That's right. And you know why? Because even though you were going through a tough time, I knew you'd come through it." He sipped his coffee. "It appears you have—which brings me to my next question. Have you given any thought to returning? You know I'd take you back in a heartbeat."

Ethan wrapped his hands around his mug. "I appreciate your confidence, but I'm committed here for the time being. Even if I weren't, I don't know if I'm ready. I enjoy what I'm doing."

"I understand. The pressures are certainly different," Stewart observed, "but you have a gift, Ethan. Whether you work for me at St. Louis Children's or go elsewhere, don't let your gift slip through your fingers."

"As I said, I'm not ready, and I don't know if I ever will be. Right now general pediatrics is enough."

"All I'm asking is for you to keep the door open to the possibility," Stewart urged. "Should you decide you're ready for a challenge of a different sort, call me. Don't talk yourself out of it because you've gotten comfortable here."

"If I decide to take the next step, I'll contact you," Ethan promised. "Until then…"

"Until then keep doing what you're doing. It's obviously working." Stewart winked.

Ethan grinned, certain Stewart had guessed that his relationship with Ivy had as much to do with his progress as returning to medicine. "It is, and I will," he promised.

Keep the door open to the possibility...should you decide you're ready for a challenge of a different sort, call me.

The sudden need for caffeine after the phone call she'd received had driven Ivy to the lounge for a bracing cup of Ethan's special blend. But she froze in her tracks as soon as she heard Stewart's voice. She hadn't meant to eavesdrop, but she couldn't backtrack until she heard Ethan's reply.

If I decide to take the next step...I'll contact you.

He'd said *if*, she told herself as she silently slipped away and sought refuge behind the battered desk that had been with her since her college days. He hadn't given a definite answer, which meant he hadn't decided one way or another. As much as she'd prepared herself for this eventuality—he only had one week to go before he fulfilled their verbal agreement—she'd selfishly hoped Ethan might choose to stay. Yet now that Stewart Trimble knew Ethan had begun to practice medicine again he'd increase the pressure on Ethan to return to St. Louis Children's Hospital.

She couldn't fault Stewart. She'd do the same thing if it meant she'd regain a top-notch neonatalogist.

The point was, however, she wouldn't be worried if she didn't have news of her own to pass along—news that could change everything and send Ethan packing by this weekend.

"Here you are." Ethan poked his head inside the room, which was hardly bigger than a closet. "I've been looking for you."

"I'm here," she said, forcing a note of cheerfulness into her voice. "Did your old boss leave?"

"Yeah. I hope you don't mind that I sent him on his way with one of your coffee mugs? He hates plastic."

If a mug was the only thing he took, she'd see that Stewart had a mug for every day of the week, in every vehicle he owned. "No problem."

Ethan moved a pile of magazines from the extra chair before he sprawled in it himself. "This has been quite a day," he mentioned.

"I'll say," she agreed fervently.

"So what did you think of Stewart?" he asked.

"He seems like a nice enough fellow. Successful, driven," she added.

"He is. I owe him a lot. He kept me sane when everything went crazy."

As much as Ivy wanted to dislike the fellow, Ethan's admission made it impossible. "I'm glad you had someone like him supporting you during that time," she said sincerely. "So, he was just passing through the area?"

"Yeah. I think he wanted to make sure I hadn't turned into a modern-day version of Jeremiah Johnson."

Ivy smiled as she remembered the old film she'd seen on a classic movie channel. The picture centered on a disenchanted veteran of the Mexican-American War who found refuge as a trapper in the mountains. "Was he pleased to find you were a productive member of society?" she teased. "Not holed up in your cabin, surrounded by empty beer bottles and pizza boxes and wearing the same clothes day in and day out?"

"He was." He paused. "He offered me a job."

"I'm not surprised. Were you?"

"No, but I told him I wasn't ready. I like what I'm doing now."

"I thought you did," she said lightly, "but it's nice hearing you say so."

"Enough about Stewart. You said earlier you had something to tell me?" He raised an expectant eyebrow.

"We have a small change in plans," she began. "Now, it doesn't have to change anything in our agreement, but it's something you should know, because it could affect our situation."

"Sounds ominous. Do you want to tell me what's going on or do I have to guess?"

Her face warmed at his wry tone. "Sorry. Jed called to tell me that Walt is back in town."

"I see. Permanently or temporarily?"

"His brother passed away last week, and Walt's home for good."

Ethan's expression remained inscrutable. "That's good. Isn't it?"

"Yes, but…" Her voice died and she drew a bracing breath. "The point is, I know we agreed you'd leave after Walt returned, but you also agreed to three weeks, which means you still have another week left. Walt's going to officially see patients on Monday, so if you want to accept Stewart's offer…"

"What do *you* want, Ivy?" he asked, rising to skirt her desk and perch on the corner next to her.

"I won't hold you to the three weeks," she said stiffly. "Walt is back, and if you want to continue with your vacation or head back to St. Louis, you can."

"What do *you* want, Ivy?" he repeated.

"It doesn't matter what I want," she said crossly. "You're the one who has to decide."

"Yes, and before I can," he said patiently, "I'd like to know your feelings on the subject."

"Oh, for heaven's sake, Ethan," she snapped. "Isn't it obvious?"

"I've learned it's best not to assume anything."

He was going to make her beg, but she wanted him so badly she would. "I want you to stay, Ethan. For however long you'd like." *A lifetime*, she wanted to add, but didn't. "I know this isn't a prestigious practice, or a booming metropolis with a convenience store on every corner, but the kids here need you."

A smile tugged at one corner of his mouth. "Only the children?"

She poured all the love she felt into her gaze. "*I* need you, Ethan, and not just as a colleague."

His smile widened. "In that case I'll stay."

It took a minute before his meaning registered. "You will?"

"For the next week," he stipulated. "That way everyone has time to adjust."

"And at the end of next week?" she pressed.

"We'll negotiate a new agreement."

"Oh?" She narrowed her eyes. "With what sort of conditions?"

"We split everything fifty-fifty," he insisted. "I'll take my share of the on-call duty, as well as the patient load."

A mental picture of Stewart formed. "What about your old boss? He doesn't seem the type to give up, and he wants you back badly."

"He'll have to learn to live with the disappointment."

"Are you certain, Ethan?" she asked. "*Absolutely* certain?"

He pulled her out of her chair and into his embrace. "I can see I'll have to show you."

Bending his head to meet her mouth, he did.

CHAPTER TEN

WALT was precisely the man Ethan had expected. Tall, thin, with sparse gray hair, twinkling eyes and a gentle smile, all combined to create a man who'd singlehandedly looked after the town's healthcare needs for years.

Until Ivy had come to lighten his load.

"I'm glad she found you to help her," Walt told him over the special dinner that Don had prepared and served to them in the small room designated for private parties. "I don't mind telling you I was worried about how she was coping."

Ivy chuckled. "I was worried about me, too. Thank goodness Ethan came to my rescue."

Ethan hadn't considered himself as a rescuer, but he basked in the light of Ivy's praise. Even if he returned to St. Louis tomorrow he wouldn't receive a reception like this, or experience the same depth of goodwill, and he was fairly envious.

"I found someone to come to mine," Walt said. "I talked Jed into staying on a couple of days a week."

"He means he twisted my arm," Jed complained good-naturedly. "But as long as I can get in a few extra days on the golf course I'll be happy."

"You never told us," Ivy exclaimed. "How wonderful!"

"I didn't want to say anything until Walt returned—" Jed said.

"What's even better," Walt interrupted, "is that between the four of us Danton won't be quite so frightening to a new physician. Not many young docs want to work like we did when we were starting out." He patted his wife's hand and exchanged a secret smile. "With any luck we'll bring in another family-practice fellow, and maybe an OB-GYN and a surgeon."

"Sounds like you have big plans," Ethan observed.

"A man has to dream big," Walt said firmly. "Otherwise his soul shrivels up and dies. It's as simple as that."

Ethan pondered Walt's philosophy long after the dinner had ended and he'd escorted Ivy home to spend the evening with her. He'd lost so much after Cody had died—a loving fiancée, a large family, a rewarding career, a place to call home. As Walt had said, without those dreams to hold on to his soul truly had shriveled and died. No wonder he'd taken to the road and drifted along without purpose.

Somehow, in her magical way, Ivy had made him want to resurrect the dreams he'd buried, but he wanted more than a resurrected dream floating in his head. He wanted to hold it within his grasp.

"You aren't paying attention to the movie," she mentioned.

"Sorry," he said. "My mind wandered."

She threaded her arm through his and snuggled against him on the sofa. "Any particular path?"

"No. I was just thinking about something Walt said."

"Dreaming big?"

He glanced at her. "How did you know?"

"He's told me that ever since I mentioned an interest in med school. 'Dream big, Ivy,' he said. 'Then go after those dreams. Most people regret the things they didn't do instead of the things they did.'"

"Sound advice."

She smiled a come-hither smile and began unbuttoning his shirt placket. "Which is why, now that you've mentioned it, I'm going to go after a particular dream of mine."

As her hands rubbed against his chest, his throat went dry. "Which is?"

"It's more in the realm of fantasy, since it involves silk scarves and honey, but we won't quibble semantics." She jumped up, then tugged him off the sofa.

"Silk and honey? This could be interesting."

"Oh, it will be," she said as she led him into the bedroom. "So don't plan on going home anytime soon."

"I won't," he promised.

The weekend went by much too fast, but it couldn't have turned out more idyllic. Fortunately she'd only gotten called to the hospital once, leaving the rest of her time free for walks in the park, a trip to the local movie theater, and just sitting on her patio enjoying the sunset.

Monday, however, rapidly went downhill—and it began with a phone call as soon as she arrived at eight.

Walt's voice came over the line. "Ivy, I need you."

The urgency in his tone immediately captured her attention. "What's up?"

"Come to the E.R. I have to deliver a pre-term baby and you have more experience with them than I do."

"We aren't set up for obstetrical services," she said cautiously.

"Ready or not, we don't have a choice. Which is why I need you here. My patient has gone into labor and I can't stop it. She's only twenty-seven weeks, Ivy. I need a pediatrician if we're going to give that youngster a fighting chance."

"How long do I have?"

"Not enough to mention."

Before she could ask another question, the dial tone hummed in her ear. *Ethan*, she thought. If a preterm infant was about to make an appearance, its best chance lay with Ethan.

She tore off down the hall, and ran into him as he was coming through the staff entrance. "It's about time you got here. We have to go."

"Go where?" he asked.

"To the E.R. Walt is about to deliver a baby and he needs our help. Actually, he needs *your* help. The baby's not full term."

"By how much?" he asked.

"Twenty-seven weeks."

Ethan let out a deep breath. "I don't suppose there's any way we can Medevac her out before she delivers?"

"No, there isn't."

"Did Walt *call* for a helicopter? Is one on its way?"

"He hung up before I could ask. We'll find out when we get there."

He followed her to the side hallway connecting the clinic to the hospital. "There isn't a lot I can do without proper tools, Ivy. Even the peds-sized equipment will be too big."

"I know, Ethan, but we have to do our best."

"You realize its chances aren't good? Not this far from a NICU."

"We can't give up without a fight."

"It will need a special airway, and an incubator or Isolette to maintain body temperature. Does the hospital even *own* one?"

"I'm not sure, but we'll make something work."

He flashed her a look of supreme disgust. "I'll bet the pharmacy doesn't even have the drugs I'll need." He froze in his tracks and met her gaze. "You do understand what I'm telling you, don't you? We're set up to fail."

Certain his complaints stemmed from insecurity, she cupped his face with both hands.

"I know this isn't an ideal situation," she said, "but I have faith in you, Ethan Locke. You may not have every gadget and high-tech gizmo you'd like at your fingertips, but *you* are that baby's best chance. Not Walt, not me. *You.* Do you hear what I'm saying?"

He nodded slowly. "I hear you."

"Good. Now, let's go."

Whether it was due to her pep talk or Ethan's instincts taking over, once they were inside his earlier hesitancy disappeared. He barked orders and sent every available nursing staff member scurrying for supplies. Technicians from the lab, respiratory services and Radiology received his instructions so they could be prepared.

"I want blood gases, glucose, calcium and bilirubin levels," he demanded. "A chest X-ray and a respirator. I don't suppose we're lucky enough to have one suitable for peds patients?"

"Actually," the respiratory therapist began, "we purchased a new unit a few months ago. With the flick of a switch it converts from adult to peds."

"What about an airway?"

"Sorry," the woman apologized. "We don't stock any as tiny as what you need."

"Damn. Well, we'll just have to improvise."

Satisfied that Ethan was organizing his end of things, Ivy went inside the trauma room, where Walt was quietly coaching his patient with her husband's help.

"How's it going?" she asked, in between the woman's contractions.

"We're having a baby soon. How're things going out there?"

"Ethan has turned into a regular Simon Legree. He's a neonatalogist, you know."

Walt's eyes widened. She'd clearly caught him off-guard with her announcement. "Well, well. At least there's one bright spot in all this."

"He's originally from St. Louis, and I'll tell you the story when this is over."

"I'll be waiting."

"In the meantime, what can I do?"

"I'll need a second pair of hands in a minute, so be ready." He addressed his patient. "Come on, Vicky. It's time for another push."

"I can't," Vicky sobbed. "The baby's coming too soon. It wasn't supposed to happen like this."

"No," Ivy agreed, "but today is your lucky day. We just happen to have a very experienced neonatalogist in town, and he's getting ready to take care of your baby as soon as it's born."

"He's a specialist?"

"That's right."

The door opened and Ethan strode in, gloved, gowned and masked, as he directed his entourage of staff.

"In fact, he's here now. So concentrate on delivering your baby."

Apparently reassured by Ethan's credentials, Vicky bore down once again. Several pushes later the head was exposed, and Walt suctioned out its nose and mouth. Another push and the shoulders slid free and into his waiting hands.

Seconds later he cut the cord and passed the baby to Ethan, who stood nearby, ready to receive the newborn baby girl who fit in the palm of one hand. He whisked her away to a radiant warmer that looked as if it should be in a museum. Regardless of its age, it worked—which was what mattered.

"Come on, darling," he coaxed as he deftly worked to make the tiny baby breathe on its own. Suddenly a weak, mewling cry came forth.

"You did it," Ivy said, amazed by Ethan's success, and relieved that he had been available to do the honors.

"Yeah," he said grimly, "but we're not out of the woods, yet. Can someone get a current ETA for the Medevac flight?"

"I'll go," a nurse volunteered, before she hurried from the room.

"What do you think?" Ivy asked him softly.

"We have a fight ahead of us. Let's hope the crew gets here with my supplies before it's too late."

"Is there anything I can do?" Ivy asked.

"Pray."

Ethan did a lot of praying himself. The supplies he'd amassed were only temporary measures. The smallest airway was too big, there wasn't an umbilical catheter anywhere to be found, and none of the staff were comfortable with handling a person who weighed in at slightly over two pounds and would have breathing difficulties. He bagged the infant himself to ensure the right amount of air got into the preemie's lungs.

"Come on, sweetheart," he coaxed. "Just hang in there for a few more minutes and then life will get better. I promise."

Suddenly a flurry of activity took place down the hall, and he breathed a sigh of relief, although he knew the real work was just beginning.

As soon as the navy blue-uniformed Medevac crew, consisting of a male nurse practitioner and a female respiratory therapist, carried in an incubator and a suitcase of supplies Ethan didn't bother with pleasantries. "I need an airway."

The respiratory therapist opened the package and held it toward him. With one smooth, practiced motion, Ethan slid it into the baby's trachea. "There, now," he soothed with his voice, aware that physical contact tended to stress premature babies rather than comfort them. "You won't have to work so hard."

Ethan continued with his tasks, inserting appropriate catheters and IV lines to carry the medication and fluids that would be required during the weeks ahead. As soon as he and the flight NP had finished administering the appropriate drugs they'd brought, Ethan placed the baby inside the warm incubator and snapped the lid closed.

"You've done this before," the nurse remarked.

Relieved that he'd performed as if he'd walked away from the NICU yesterday, rather than over six months ago, Ethan managed a smile. "Children's Hospital, St. Louis."

"It's lucky you were here," the fellow said. "We don't often take one back this small, or in such relatively good condition."

"Yeah, lucky thing," Ethan echoed. "Keep me posted, will you?"

"Here's our card," he said, and he handed one to Ethan. "The number listed is a direct line to the NICU."

"Thanks."

Within a few minutes Ethan's small patient had left. Surprisingly enough, by the time he'd stripped off his protective gear and found Ivy at the nurses' station with Walt, he felt a disquieting sense of loss. He simply wasn't accustomed to handing his patients to someone else. Normally he was the one who received them for the long haul, and in turn they'd become "his" kids.

Yet he'd left that life behind, so those feelings were inappropriate—weren't they?

"Everyone deserves a commendation," Ivy declared, her eyes sparkling with happiness. "You, Walt, for delivering a baby when it's been years since you've done so—"

"Let's hope it won't happen again before I retire," the older man said fervently, craning his neck in an obvious attempt to work out the kinks.

"And you, Ethan—" Ivy turned toward him "—deserve one for keeping that baby alive without proper equipment. You were utterly and amazingly fantastic."

He grinned. "Just what I like to hear. Undying praise."

"I'm serious. I couldn't have done what you did."

"You'd be surprised what you can accomplish when you don't have a choice," he said. "I have a suggestion, though. Even if we don't routinely offer obstetric services, there will be times, like today, when we will. In order to be properly prepared we need supplies on hand for a preemie, as well as a term infant. If the helicopter hadn't arrived when it did, the story could have ended differently."

"I'll talk to the nursing director right away," Ivy promised.

"Good, because, for the record, I hate improvising. By the way, where's the mother? I didn't get a chance to visit with her."

"She's on her way to Wichita by ambulance," Walt said. "Other than going into labor early, she doesn't seem to have any problems. I only wish she hadn't waited to come in. I might have been able to stop her contractions completely, or at least for long enough to ship her out so she could have had her baby elsewhere."

"Unfortunately we have to play the cards we're dealt," Ethan mentioned. "We got them both this far. The rest is up to the specialists in Wichita." For an instant he felt an overriding sense of jealousy, then told himself he was being ridiculous.

Walt rose and stretched. "Such drama so early in the morning. I feel like I've put in a full day's work, and it's barely ten o'clock."

"Stop by our place for Ethan's special blend of gourmet coffee," Ivy suggested. "There's enough caffeine in one cup to turn you into the Energizer Bunny."

"Hey," Ethan protested without heat. "Are you complaining about my nectar of the gods?"

"Whatever you call it, I can use a tall one with extra sugar." Walt clapped Ethan on his back. "In case I forgot to tell you the other night, welcome aboard."

"Thanks. I have to say, there's never a dull moment around here."

Walt nodded soberly. "Never has been and never will be. A smart man will buckle in and hang on for the ride."

If Walt's experience had drained him, by his own admission Ethan claimed the opposite. He hadn't felt this energized in months. Yet, in spite of the adrenalin rush caused by his apparent success, and in spite of how skills that had once been second nature had surfaced when he needed them, he hadn't forgotten how easily the situation could have turned into his worst nightmare instead of a celebration. As he'd groused to Ivy beforehand, he hadn't had the proper equipment or specially trained staff during that first crucial hour or so before the experienced flight team had arrived.

While the "what ifs" sent a chill down his spine when he reflected on them, he found himself wondering all day what interventions and treatments the neonatalogist in Wichita was implementing. He began watching the clock, guessing at what the NICU staff a hundred and fifty miles away would be doing. He wanted to phone the number on the business card and ask for a status report, but, having been on the other side, as an attending physician who hated interruptions before he'd had time to do his job, Ethan forced himself to wait.

By five o'clock it seemed safe to call.

As soon as he identified himself the neonatalogist's voice warmed, and he rattled off the baby's problems and treatment in familiar lingo. Poor respiratory effort headed the list, but that was only to be expected.

By the time Ethan broke the connection he was grinning like a loon and feeling immensely satisfied at his role in the morning's drama.

"You're looking rather pleased with yourself," said Ivy.

"I just talked to the NICU about baby girl Jarrett," Ethan admitted. "She's behaving like a little lady and not throwing any big surprises at the staff." He grinned.

"I'm glad," she said simply. "After seeing you in action, I can understand why Stewart wants you back."

He dismissed her comment. "Stewart's prejudiced. He hates it when any of his staff leaves."

"Probably, but people with your skill don't grow on trees, Ethan. You managed the impossible without proper equipment, which tells me you can move mountains when you have it."

The one mountain he'd wanted to move more than anything had refused to budge, no matter how hard he'd tried. "I couldn't save my son," he reminded her.

"But you did everything possible," she insisted. "Sometimes what's possible isn't enough. In another ten years who knows how far science will have progressed? Meanwhile, we aren't there yet, no matter how badly we want it."

She'd offered the same argument Stewart had presented time after time, but guilt was stronger than logic.

"You didn't fail your son, Ethan, because some things are simply out of your hands. Forgive your profession for not being as advanced as you needed it to be. Concentrate on what you *can* do with the knowledge we have so far. That was the knowledge you used to save the Jarrett baby, as well as every baby before her and every child who will come after her."

Her argument made sense, and because it did the day's experience demanded that he take a fresh look at his life and re-evaluate what he wanted. At the moment, though, he was basking in the afterglow of success. Decisions could come later.

He drew her into his arms. "How did you get to be so wise?"

"I was born that way," she said pertly as she tucked her head underneath his chin. "Are you ready to put the day behind you and rest on your laurels?"

He laughed. "I don't claim any laurels, but, yeah, I'm ready to decompress."

"Good, because I know this great little place for dinner. No reservations required."

Ivy had always considered her sixth sense to be a blessing, and she'd learned to rely on those instincts. Now those instincts didn't comfort her at all.

After watching Ethan work on the Jarrett baby she knew beyond all doubt that he didn't belong in Danton, treating nosebleeds and strep throat. He belonged in a highly specialized environment where he could give hope to the hopeless.

It had taken every ounce of fortitude to talk to him about his skills when she really wanted to ignore everything she'd seen. Unfortunately, ignoring the obvious wouldn't make it disappear. Ethan might believe he'd be content sharing her practice, and perhaps he would be for a while, but he was destined for greater things. He might not realize it today, but he was a smart, intuitive man. One day soon he'd realize that settling for second best wasn't the answer.

For the next few days Ivy pretended that life was perfect. She joked and teased and acted as if she didn't have a care in world. Underneath though, her heart was breaking.

Although Ethan hadn't said a word, she knew his former career was whispering his name. He phoned the NICU daily for updates on Lacey Jarrett, and he'd had a lengthy conversation with Stewart on Thursday.

As further evidence, he seemed more quiet and introspective, and at times she caught him studying her as if he were memorizing her features.

He would be leaving soon. Although he hadn't mentioned the possibility, she knew it deep in her bones. The only question was when?

For the third night in a row, Ethan tossed and turned before finally dozing off in the wee hours of the morning. His thoughts of Ivy intertwined with thoughts about his future until he felt as if he were stuck on a hamster wheel and couldn't free himself.

But, in spite of his dilemma, he knew what he had to do. "Dream big" Walt had told him. Well, he'd dusted off those dreams of a wife, family and a career he loved, and now he held them in front of him. Each one was attainable, but before he could work toward the two he craved the most he had to sort out his career—because it had affected and would continue to influence the others.

He didn't object to working with Ivy in her clinic, but after treating the Jarrett baby he realized that he missed the challenges of the profession he'd once loved. After losing his son he'd become disillusioned, but, as Ivy had reminded him, medicine wasn't yet a perfect science, no matter how much he wanted to believe it was. Tiffany might hold him responsible for the loss of their son, and he would always mourn for the little boy who'd died before he had a chance to live, but beating himself up over circumstances he couldn't control wasn't the answer. He had to move on.

He *wanted* to move on.

Unfortunately doing so meant he had to walk away from

Ivy. It would be easier to rip out his heart, which was why he'd directed their conversations these past few days toward superficial or work-related topics and away from personal ones. Sadly enough, being lighthearted didn't stop him from feeling guilty over the way he'd leave her when she'd been counting on his help.

He had to tell her, and soon.

Oh, how he hated goodbyes. It would have been easier if Ivy had remained a colleague or an acquaintance, but she'd become so much more. She'd literally saved him from himself. How could he possibly expect to walk away without wrenching his heart?

He'd tell her on Friday, after Italian night at the diner. She and her father were already gearing up for the event, and they didn't need the distraction of knowing he would drive away in a couple of days.

Friday night. He'd pack all the memories he could into the next twenty-four hours and hope they'd be enough to sustain him.

"What's my job, boss?" Ethan asked on Friday night, before Don opened the doors to the public.

Ivy smiled. Ethan had insisted on coming to the diner with her, but she hadn't expected him to work. "Are you serious?"

"I wouldn't have offered otherwise," he said. "Besides, *you're* helping. Why can't I?"

Ivy had donned the required waitress uniform for the evening, which consisted of black jeans, a white shirt and a black vest. "It's my dad's business. I *have* to help. Honestly, I didn't think you'd want to get your hands dirty."

"You were wrong. For the record, though, I have busboy experience."

He looked like a little boy who was eager to play. "I

suppose it wouldn't hurt if we had two instead of one." Ivy adjusted a red checkered tablecloth.

Don passed by on his way to turn over the sign in the window from Closed to Open. "I have a better idea. Ethan, you can be in charge of the coffee and carry heavy trays of food to the table, so the girls won't have to. How does that sound?"

"Perfect."

"Good. Then grab an apron and get ready."

As customers began streaming into the diner, Ivy began taking orders. After a while she devised a system for Ethan to follow. She raised her hand and snapped her fingers to grab his attention, then held up the appropriate number of digits to indicate how many cups were requested at each table.

Her system generated a lot of teasing comments, but Ethan took them in stride.

"I'll get you for this," he threatened good-naturedly, when he met her in the kitchen to carry out a large serving tray of spaghetti to a party of six.

Ivy laughed. "Promises, promises."

As the evening wore on, she noticed how easily he visited with everyone in town. He'd changed completely from the man who'd first huddled in the corner by himself, avoiding everyone and dining alone. The image of him as he served her father's clientele, clad in a white "Don's Diner" apron and looking as if he were enjoying himself, wouldn't ever leave her.

Maybe he wasn't leaving, she considered hopefully. He hadn't said a word, and surely he wouldn't drive away without a goodbye of some sort? Even as she clung to the thought she knew she was only fooling herself.

How could she let him go?

She didn't have a choice.

Fortunately, the steady crowd kept her from dwelling on a situation that was out of her control. Even after the hordes of hungry people had cleared out, the usual closing tasks of filling condiment shakers, sanitizing tables and sweeping the floor occupied her mind, as well as her hands, until finally Don sent them home.

"We should start a campaign to raise the tip percentage waitresses earn," Ethan said as he ushered her to his car. "They need it just to replace their shoes."

"Remember that the next time you visit a restaurant."

"Trust me, I will."

After a short, silent drive, he escorted her to her front door. "Would you like to come in?" she asked.

He didn't hesitate. "Yes, I would."

His expression seemed far too serious for this time of night, and her instincts warned her to brace herself. With a troubled heart, she led the way inside.

Although she wasn't thirsty, she needed a task to occupy her hands. "I'm going to fix a pot of coffee. Want some?"

"Sure. We had quite a crowd tonight, didn't we?"

She measured the grounds, poured water into the reservoir and flicked the switch. "We did," she agreed. "I'll be curious to know if we topped our last event in sales." She rubbed her neck. "It certainly feels like we did."

"Your dad should bottle his homemade sauce and sell it in gourmet food stores. He'd make a small fortune in the city."

"I'll tell him. He'll be flattered you think it's good enough to compete." She filled two mugs and set them on the table.

"If it's something he'd like to pursue, I know some people who—"

"Ethan," she said softly, "you didn't come here to devise a marketing plan for my dad's Italian sauce."

"You know me too well," he said wryly.

"You want to tell me something, don't you?"

He frowned. "How did you know?"

"I've suspected it all week," she said, gripping her mug with both hands as if it were a lifeline. "You're leaving, aren't you?"

He pressed his mouth into a hard line, and with apologetic eyes he nodded. "Yeah."

"When?" She braced herself for his answer.

"In the morning."

CHAPTER ELEVEN

Ivy was pleased she sounded so normal when she was screaming inside. "So soon?"

"It seemed best. Postponing would only make leaving more difficult than it already is." He paused. "Stewart's expecting me on Monday. I'm already packed."

He'd already packed? She wanted to toss something at him for not telling her until the last minute, but she would be adult about this even if it killed her.

"Any reason why you waited until now to tell me?" she asked calmly. "Were you afraid I'd talk you out of going?"

"No. I just didn't want to hurt you and I knew I would."

"I see." She rose to dump her mug's contents down the drain before she flung them at him.

"I have to leave, Ivy. I realized on Monday that I can't go forward without first going back."

As painful as his comment was, he was right. "I know," she whispered.

He joined her near the sink and took her hands in his. "I want to thank you for everything. For trusting in me, for listening." He lowered his head to kiss her.

As soon as his mouth met hers she was lost.

"Don't go," she begged.

"Oh, Ivy—" he began, his voice filled with regret.

"For tonight," she corrected herself. "I know you're leaving, but stay the night. Save your goodbye until morning. Please?"

His eyes filled with a combination of hunger and need, and she guessed he saw the same in hers. "OK," he said. "I'll stay."

Ivy concentrated on the man and forced herself not to think about how this evening marked the last time for so many things. The last time she'd see him in her bed; the last time they'd eat together at the diner; the last time she'd see him in the hallway or smell his special brand of soap.

No regrets, she reminded herself, before he carried her to the stars and she slowly drifted back to earth.

Silently he tucked her close, and she dozed, content in his warm embrace. It was hard to say how long she slept, but a small rustle of clothing brought her awake. His side of the bed was empty, and only the impression of his head on the pillow marked his presence.

He was getting dressed in the dark. She waited for him to speak, mainly because she couldn't force a word past the lump in her throat.

Suddenly the bed dipped in his direction and she felt his lips brush against her forehead. Then he was gone.

When she heard the quiet snick of her door closing, tears streamed down her face. "He didn't say goodbye," she whispered to her pillow.

Then again, he just did.

Three weeks later Ivy sat in the diner, nursing a piece of peanut butter pie and a cup of coffee under her father's watchful eye.

"You don't look so good," he said bluntly.

"Thanks, Dad," she said wryly. "But if I recall, we've had this conversation before."

"You're working too hard."

"No worse than usual." Although some of her peds patients had gone back to Walt, she was busy enough that she hadn't actually noticed. It was just as well, because keeping busy kept her mind off Ethan during the day.

If only she could drive him out of her thoughts at night, because then it was impossible.

After clinging to his pillow and breathing in his residual scent all night after he'd left, she'd gotten up, stripped the bed and replaced her pillows. Then she'd gone to her office, thrown out every trace of his gourmet coffee grounds and sanitized each room. By the time she'd left her patient rooms and the lounge had smelled like hospital-strength disinfectant.

"Have you heard from Ethan?"

"He sent a package the other day." She'd received it three days and five hours ago.

"Oh?"

"He sent preemie-sized supplies to have on hand just in case." As crazy as it sounded, she'd kept his note until this morning, because seeing his bold scrawl made him seem nearby. It wasn't enough that she saw his handwriting in her patient charts, she had to torture herself with his extra note.

"That was nice," her father remarked.

Ivy shrugged. "I don't know who he thinks will use them. As far as I'm concerned he wasted his time and his money."

"You should have asked him to stay."

"It wouldn't have mattered," she said wearily. "He needed to go. We both knew that."

"Maybe he'll be back."

"Maybe, but I doubt it."

"Why? You meant a lot to him." He peered at her. "I'm guessing the feeling ran both ways."

"We belong in different worlds, Dad. It's as simple as that. Ethan moved on with his life and I need to do the same."

Unfortunately, some things were easier said than done.

In spite of his welcome back to the NICU, and Stewart letting him move into his basement until he found something more permanent, Ethan still felt as if something were missing. He'd realized it as soon as he'd passed the Danton city-limit sign.

He missed Ivy.

He missed her smile, the way she looked at him as if he were her hero, the way she was too generous for her own good. In fact, he missed everything about her.

Fortunately the NICU had been as busy as he remembered, which helped in that regard, although at times he had trouble glancing at the Isolette in the corner where his son had been. But, no matter how busy his days were, his nights dragged on until he thought he'd go mad if he didn't hear her voice.

He'd hoped she'd call when she received his package, but she hadn't. Instead, the nursing director had written a note thanking him for his generous gift.

He didn't blame Ivy for keeping her distance, but he wanted her in his life as much as a plant needed sunshine. There had to be a way....

Dream big.

Walt's words echoed in his head. OK, he decided, he would.

Suddenly the floodgates burst open, and he knew how he could give his dreams substance. It took another month to set his plan in motion, but this time when he left St. Louis he was excited about the future.

He was going home.

* * *

"Someone's waiting to see you, Ivy," Heather said.

Ivy groaned. "A patient?"

"No. A fellow. Nice-looking, too."

"Oh, for heaven's sake," Ivy complained. "It's after six on a Friday evening. Now isn't the time for a drug rep to pay a courtesy call."

Heather shrugged. "Do you want me to get rid of him for you?"

Considering she would be going to the diner for another lonely meal in a long line of lonely meals, then home for a weekend of house-cleaning and laundry, what did it matter if she postponed her exciting schedule for a few minutes? "No, I'll see what he wants," she said wearily.

"Great. Enjoy your two days off."

"Yeah, right."

Ivy pinched the bridge of her nose, then strode down the hallway to deal with the man who had the audacity to show up after office hours.

"I'm Dr. Harris," she told the man who was studying the prints on her wall—a man whose build and hair coloring reminded her of Ethan's. "What can I do for you?"

He turned, and she gasped.

"Ethan?" she asked, incredulous.

He smiled. "In the flesh."

"What— When— What are you doing here? Heather didn't say a word." Her eyes narrowed. "She was in on this, wasn't she?"

"In a way. I bribed her with two tickets to a country music concert in Wichita."

"Only two? I'm surprised she went so cheap."

He shrugged. "What can I say? She likes me."

Along with everyone else in town, she thought, with some disgust. Everyone in town had gotten the idea she'd sent him away instead of him leaving on his own. "Why are you here, Ethan?"

"Rumor says you're looking for a partner."

"I am." She was suspicious.

"I'm here to submit my curriculum vitae for consideration."

She couldn't have heard correctly. "You?"

"Yes. I'm certified in pediatrics, and—"

"You don't have to recite your credentials, Ethan. I know what they are. However, I'm not looking for a neonatalogist."

He stepped closer. "Too bad. Because there's one thing in particular I never told you. One thing that might convince you to change your mind."

"Which is?"

"I'm the man who loves you, Ivy," he said simply.

"You…love me?" Her surprise gave way to anger. "How can you say that? You left almost two months ago, after stealing away in the middle of the night. Two months, Ethan. Two months without a phone call or a letter. Just a note in a package of medical equipment that said, 'with compliments'."

"I didn't know how to tell you. Then, once I took Walt's advice to dream big, I knew I had to wait until I could tell you in person."

She sank onto a chair. "Oh, Ethan. I love you, too, but I don't see how we can make it work. I can't leave, and there's nothing for you here. And don't tell me you're willing to give up your specialty because I won't let you."

He sat beside her. "That's why it took me so long before I could come back. I've signed a contract with a locum tenens agency, and I'm already booked for two weeks a month. That means I can spend the other two weeks in Danton, working with you."

"You did what?" she screeched.

"I'm officially a locum tenens," he explained patiently. "I'm contracted for—"

"No, I heard that. I just can't believe it."

"Believe it, Ivy. I've sorted out my career so I can have the best of both worlds. Now I want to sort out the rest of my dreams." His gaze grew intent enough to send a shiver of anticipation down Ivy's spine.

"And they are?"

"Marry me, Ivy. I can't promise I'll be the best husband there ever was, and with my job you'll be on your own at various times, but I'll always be your colleague, your partner and your lover. I'll even be your father's busboy, coffee-server and general dogsbody on occasion."

She giggled through the happy tears clogging her throat.

"I want you as my wife, Ivy. It's as simple as that."

"Oh, Ethan," she breathed.

"When I left town I wanted to turn around and ask you to wait for me. But I knew it wouldn't be right. Now, though, it is. I didn't run away this time, Ivy. I ran toward you."

Tears glistened in her eyes. "I'd be honored to marry you, Ethan Locke, because I love you more than you can imagine. I'll always be your colleague, your partner and your lover. I'll support you, be your helpmate, and I will also let you be my father's busboy on occasion."

He laughed. "Shall we tell your dad the good news?"

"Later," she said with a warm smile as she tugged him out of his chair. "Much, much later. In fact, he just might have to wait until tomorrow, because I intend to welcome you home properly."

"Hmm. What exactly does a proper welcome include?"

"Lots of love."

FREE

2 BOOKS AND A SURPRISE GIFT!

We would like to take this opportunity to thank you for reading this Mills & Boon® book by offering you the chance to take TWO more specially selected titles from the Medical™ series absolutely FREE! We're also making this offer to introduce you to the benefits of the Mills & Boon® Book Club™ —

- ★ **FREE home delivery**
- ★ **FREE gifts and competitions**
- ★ **FREE monthly Newsletter**
- ★ **Books available before they're in the shops**
- ★ **Exclusive Mills & Boon Book Club offers**

Accepting these FREE books and gift places you under no obligation to buy; you may cancel at any time, even after receiving your free shipment. Simply complete your details below and return the entire page to the address below. You don't even need a stamp!

YES! Please send me 2 free Medical books and a surprise gift. I understand that unless you hear from me, I will receive 4 superb new titles every month for just £2.99 each, postage and packing free. I am under no obligation to purchase any books and may cancel my subscription at any time. The free books and gift will be mine to keep in any case.

M9ZEE

Ms/Mrs/Miss/Mr.............................Initials ....
BLOCK CAPITALS PLEASE

Surname ....

Address ....

....

....Postcode ....

Send this whole page to:
The Mills & Boon Book Club, FREEPOST CN81, Croydon, CR9 3WZ